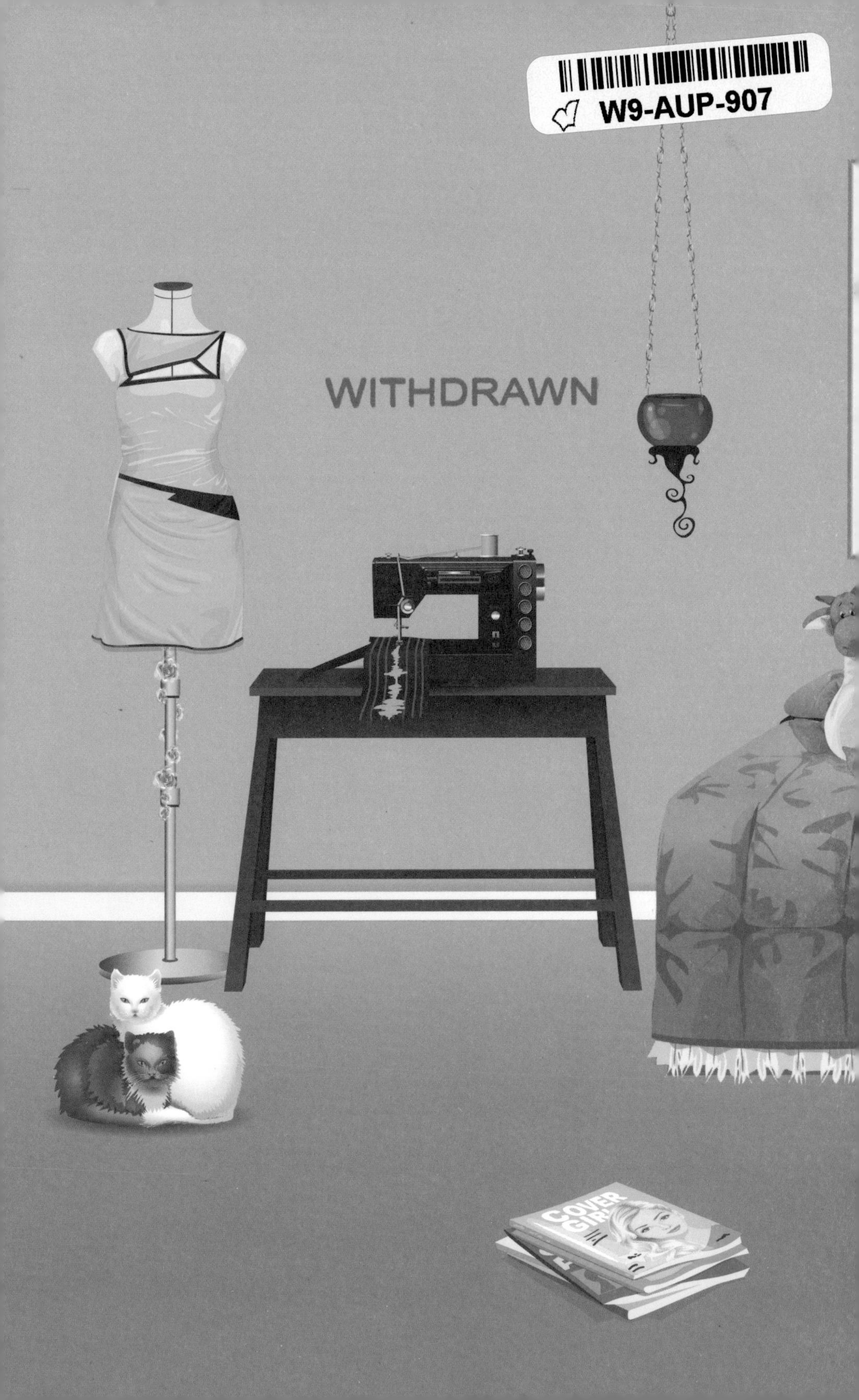
COVER

stardoll™

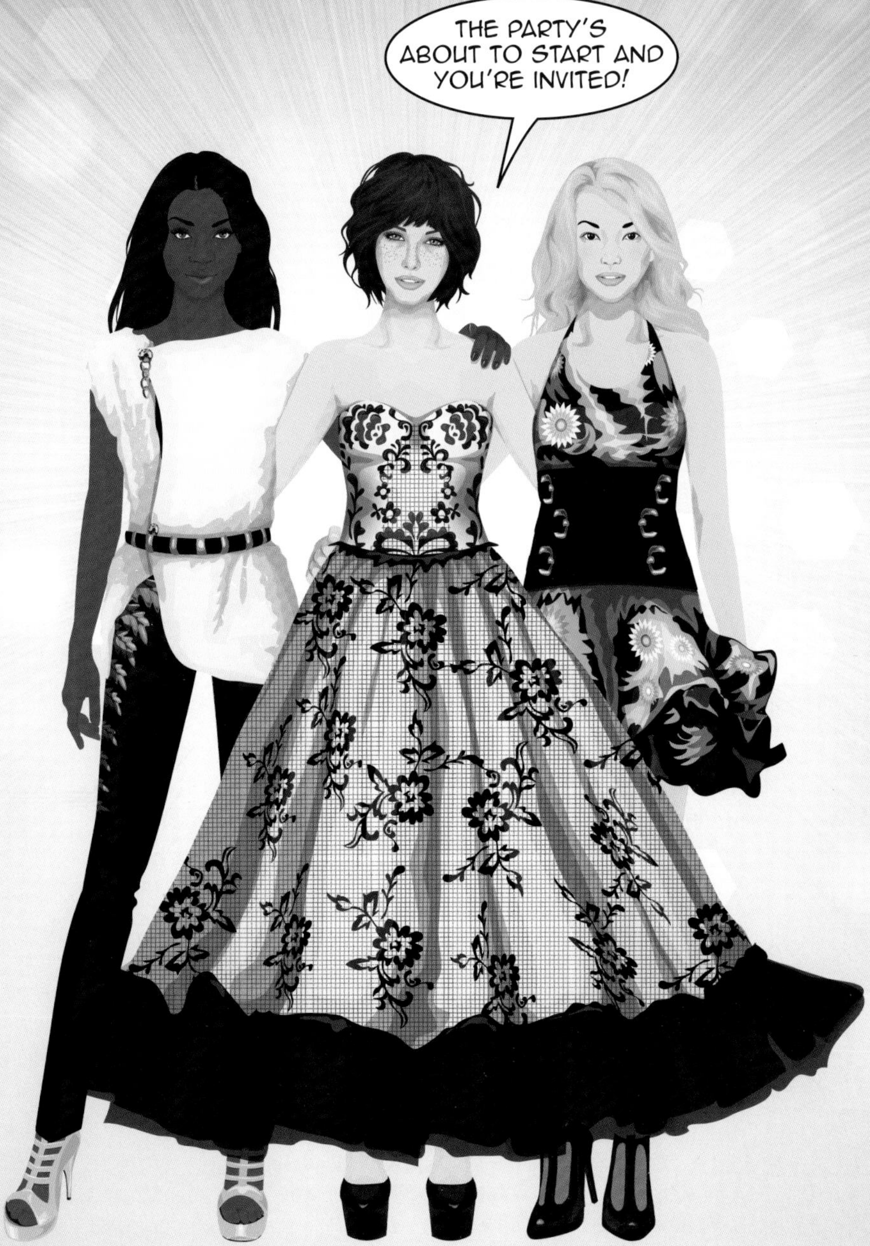
THE PARTY'S ABOUT TO START AND YOU'RE INVITED!

PAPERCUTZ™

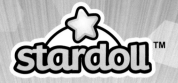

stardoll™

Graphic Novels Available from

PAPERCUTZ™

stardoll
Secrets & Dreams
by JayJay Jackson
PAPERCUTZ

STARDOLL
Graphic Novel #1
"SECRETS & DREAMS"

stardoll
The Secret of the Star Jewel
by JayJay Jackson
PAPERCUTZ

COMING SOON!
Graphic Novel #2
"THE SECRET OF THE STAR JEWEL"

STARDOLL graphic novels, the print editions, are available at booksellers everywhere.

Or order directly from Papercutz. STARDOLL available in paperback for $7.99 each; in hardcover for $11.99 each. Please add $4.00 for postage and handling for the first book, and add $1.00 for each additional book.

Make check payable to NBM Publishing.
Send to: Papercutz, 160 Broadway, Suite 700, East Wing, New York, NY 10038
Or call 800-886-1223 between 9-5 EST, M-F. Visa, MC, and AmEx accepted.

www.papercutz.com

STARDOLL graphic novels are also available digitally wherever e-books are sold.

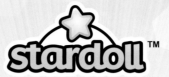

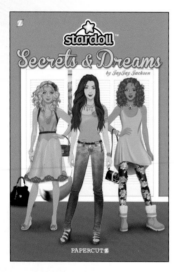

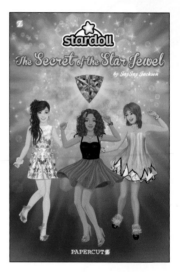

stardoll™

Secrets & Dreams

JAYJAY JACKSON – Writer & Artist

PAPERCUTZ™

NEW YORK

STARDOLL is a virtual paper doll community site for everyone who enjoys fame, fashion and friends – and the inspiration for this series of graphic novels by JayJay Jackson. At stardoll.com you can create your own MeDoll or choose from an ever-growing collection of celebrity dolls and dress them up in a wide selection of fashions. Every celebrity doll has a wardrobe full of unique clothes and there are new dolls released every week. The non-superstar membership is free.

Stardoll's original name was Paperdollheaven.com, and started out as the hobby of the Scandinavian-born Liisa. Inspired by a childhood passion for paper dolls, Liisa started drawing dolls and accompanying wardrobes and taught herself web design. Her personal homepage rapidly became a popular destination for teens. In 2004, with the help of her son, she upgraded the site and called it Paperdoll Heaven.

Stardoll is one of few places on the Internet developed with an emphasis on girls' self-expression through fantasy and fashion play. Stardoll.com is a great place to spend time with friends and to meet other kids from all over the world. It's an inspiring, safe and creative environment. "Most online sites are focused on violence and competitiveness," says Liisa. "I wanted to create a positive online environment for young girls who are creative and interested in fashion. They are looking for alternatives to shoot 'em up and kill 'em games." Liisa is still an important part of the Stardoll family and she makes new paper dolls every week.

STARDOLL
#1 "Secrets & Dreams"
JayJay Jackson – Writer, Artist, Colorist, Letterer
Special thanks to Jim Shooter, James Fry and Joe James for all of their help!
And thank you to Ashley Skeels, Ruby Claire Roessler, Trish Aponte, and Sue-Ni DiStefano.
JayJay Jackson – Design & Production
Beth Scorzato – Production Coordinator
Associate Editor – Michael Petranek
Jim Salicrup
Editor-in-Chief

ISBN: 978-1-59707-418-6 paperback edition
ISBN: 978-1-59707-419-3 hardcover edition

Printed in Canada
July 2013 by Friesens Printing
1 Printers Way
Altona, MB ROG OBO

Papercutz books may be purchased for business or promotional use.
For information on bulk purchases please contact Macmillan Corporate
and Premium Sales Department at (800) 221-7945 x5442.

Distributed by Macmillan
First Printing

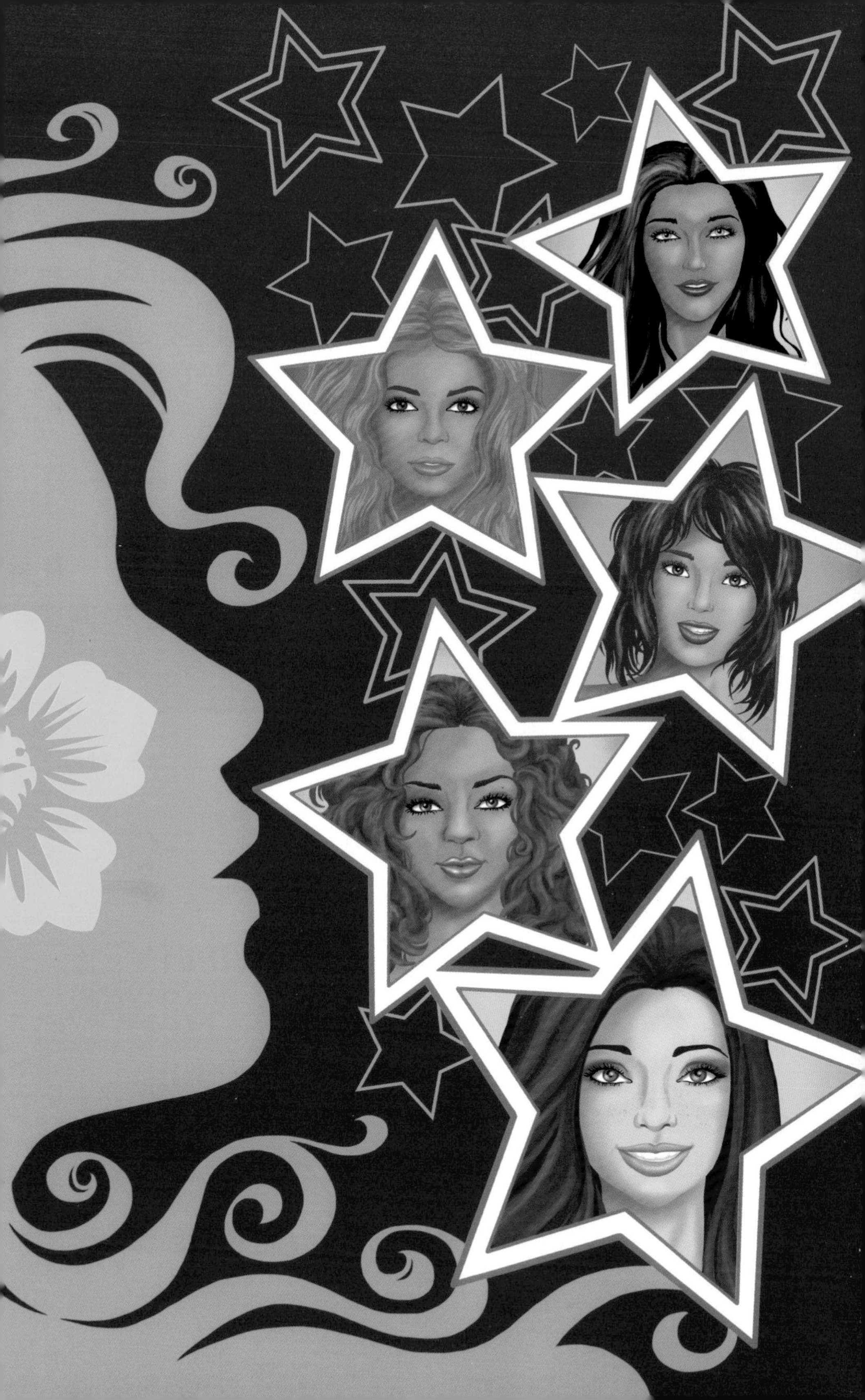

Los Angeles High School of Fashion and Design

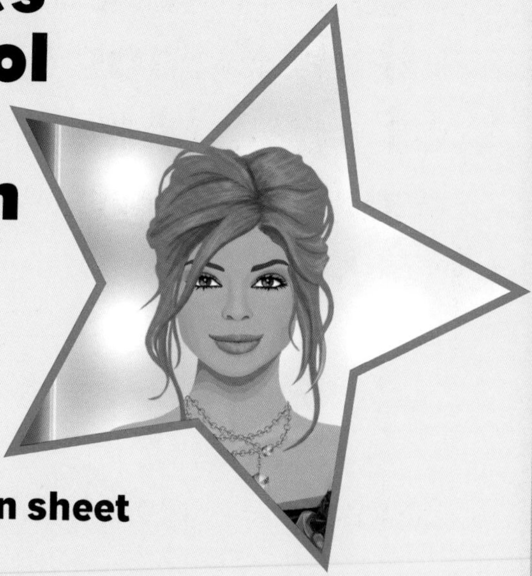

Student information sheet

Name: Ashley Archer

Eye Color: Brown

Hair Color: Dark Blonde

Fashion Style: Feminine, Athletic

Goals: Fashion business management

Interests: Parkour, Capoeira, Extreme Sports

Other: "Always do what is right. It will gratify half of mankind and astound the other." - Mark Twain

Los Angeles High School of Fashion and Design

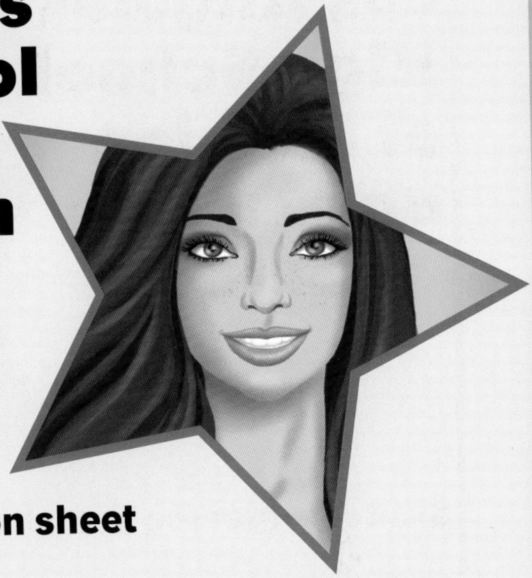

Student information sheet

Name: *Claire Leo*

Eye Color: *Blue*

Hair Color: *Deep Auburn*

Fashion Style: *Casual, Fashion Forward*

Goals: *Fashion designer*

Interests: *Drawing, Sewing, Pattern making*

Other: *I have two cats. Their names are Chloé and Chanel*

Los Angeles High School of Fashion and Design

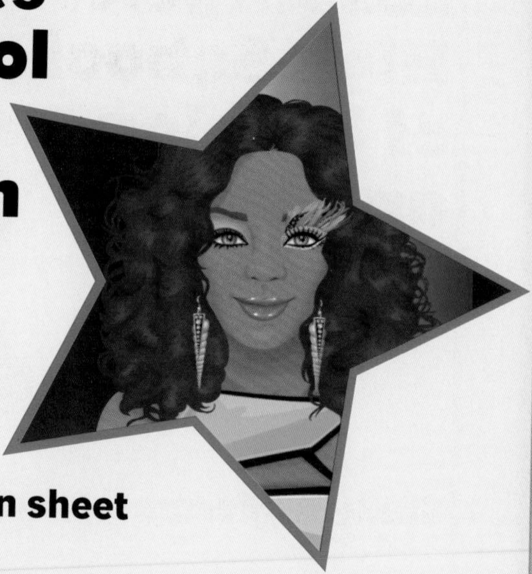

Student information sheet

Name: Kaya Reynard

Eye Color: Gold

Hair Color: Rich Bright Auburn

Fashion Style: Eclectic, Urban

Goals: Interior Designer

Interests: Family and friends, socializing

Other: I love to create look books out of fashion magazines.

Los Angeles High School of Fashion and Design

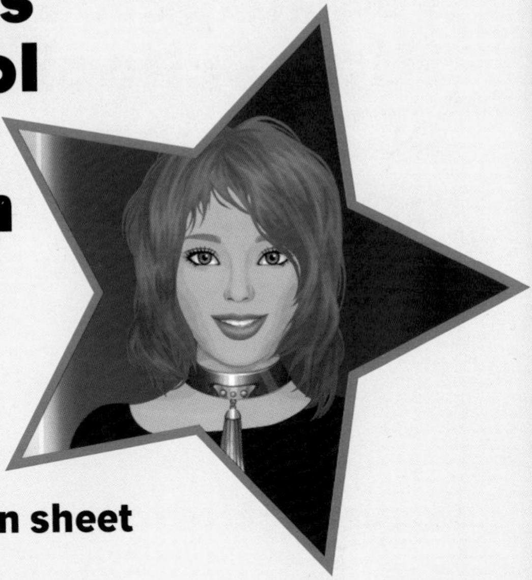

Student information sheet

Name: *Ruby Zara*

Eye Color: *Grey*

Hair Color: *Changeable*

Fashion Style: *80s Vintage, Geek Chic*

Goals: *Fashion Technology*

Interests: *Internet, Technology, Cultural Studies*

Other: *My Faves: Dancing to 80s music, watching John Hughes movies.*

Los Angeles High School of Fashion and Design

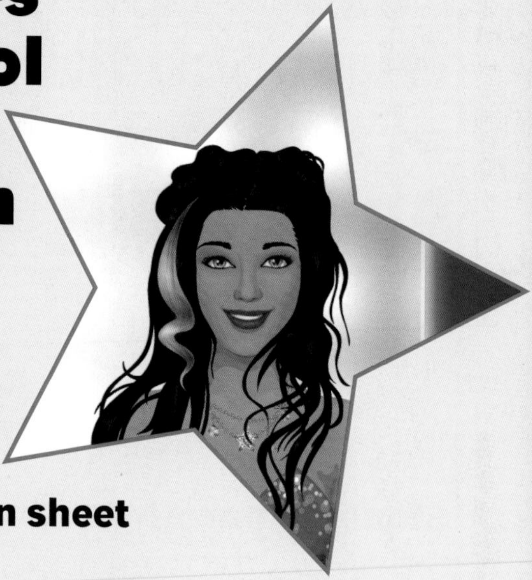

Student information sheet

Name: Sue-Ni MacDuffie

Eye Color: Aquamarine

Hair Color: Black with an aqua streak

Fashion Style: Pretty, Asian inspired

Goals: Fashion Buyer

Interests: Bollywood Dance, Swimming, Shopping

Other: Guilty pleasures: Romance novels and Bollywood musicals

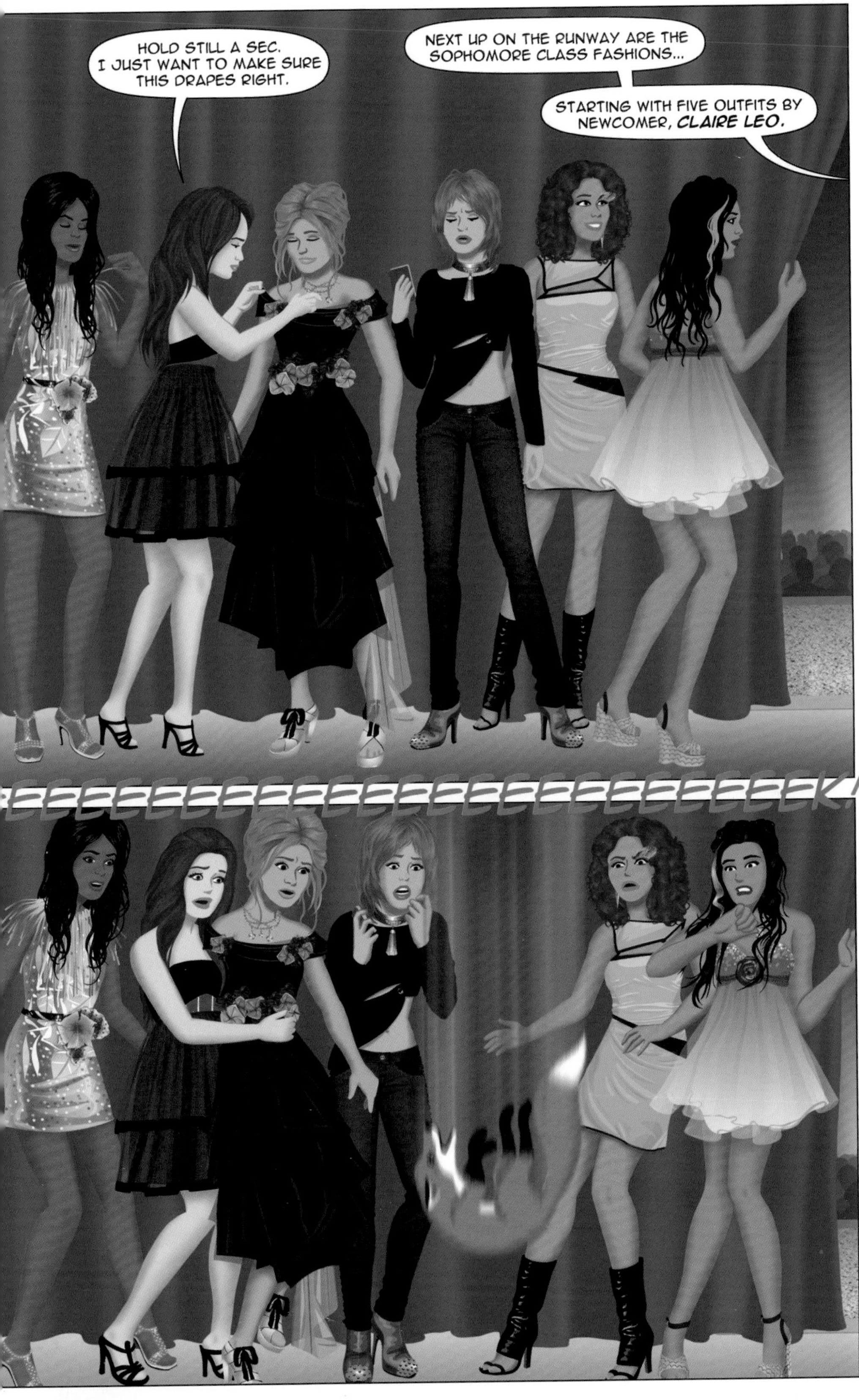
HOLD STILL A SEC. I JUST WANT TO MAKE SURE THIS DRAPES RIGHT.
NEXT UP ON THE RUNWAY ARE THE SOPHOMORE CLASS FASHIONS...
STARTING WITH FIVE OUTFITS BY NEWCOMER, ***CLAIRE LEO.***
EEEEEEEEEEEEEEEEEEEEEEEK!

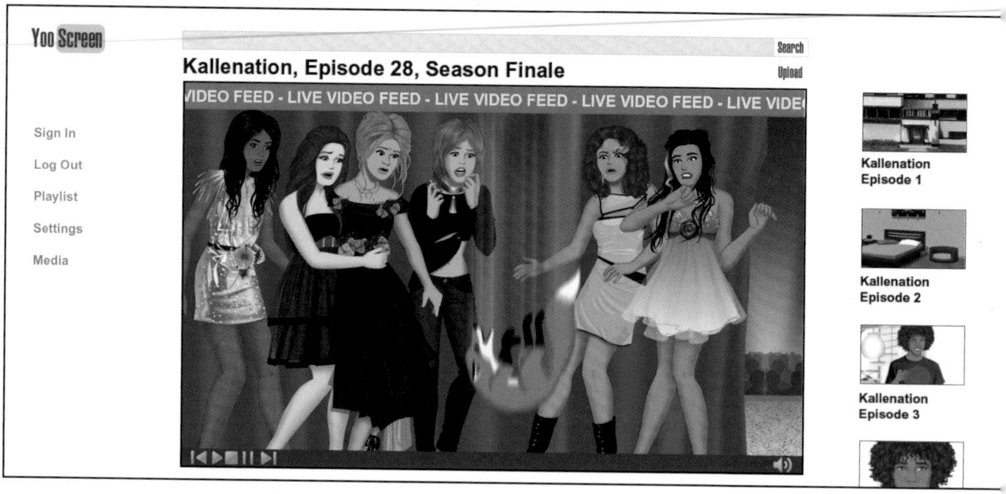

Yoo Screen
Search
Kallenation, Episode 28, Season Finale
Upload
VIDEO FEED - LIVE VIDEO FEED - LIVE VIDEO FEED - LIVE VIDEO FEED - LIVE VIDEO
Sign In
Log Out
Playlist
Settings
Media
Kallenation Episode 1
Kallenation Episode 2
Kallenation Episode 3

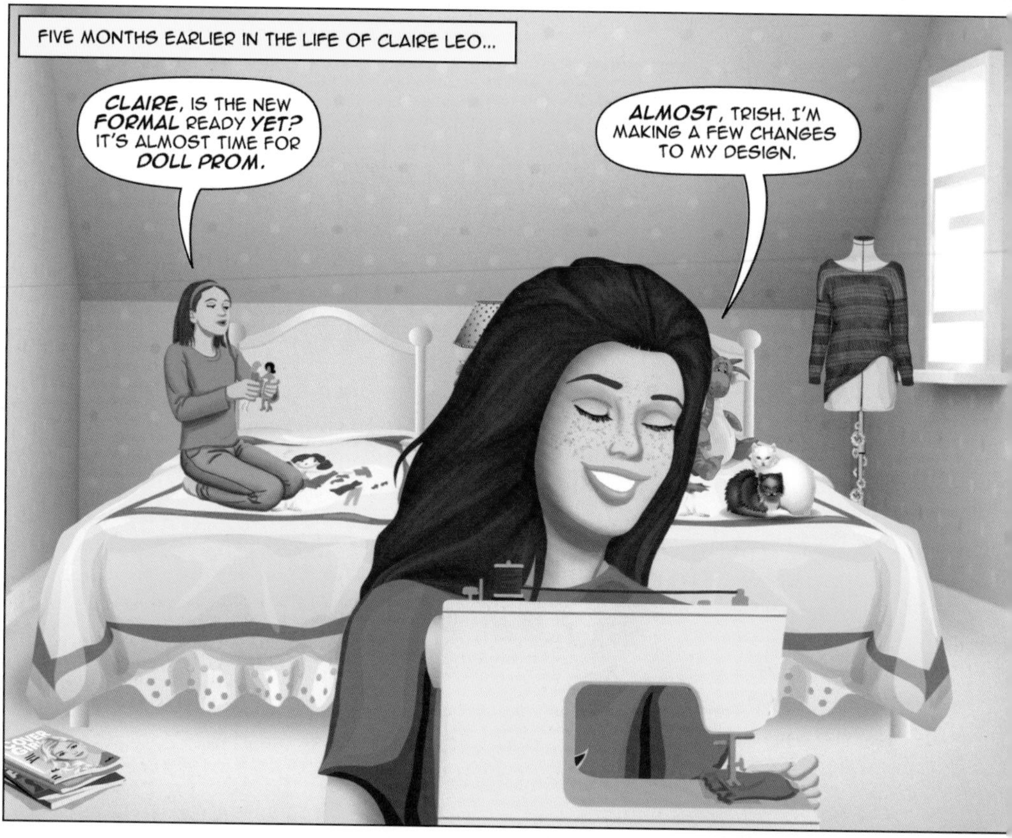

FIVE MONTHS EARLIER IN THE LIFE OF CLAIRE LEO...
CLAIRE, IS THE NEW FORMAL READY YET? IT'S ALMOST TIME FOR DOLL PROM.
ALMOST, TRISH. I'M MAKING A FEW CHANGES TO MY DESIGN.

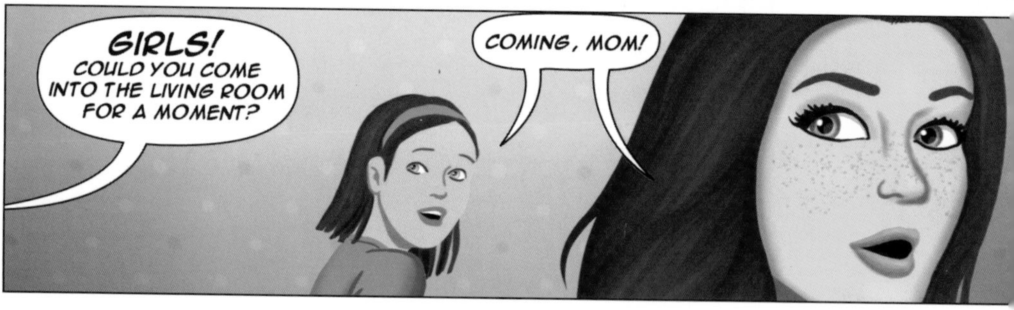

GIRLS! COULD YOU COME INTO THE LIVING ROOM FOR A MOMENT?
COMING, MOM!

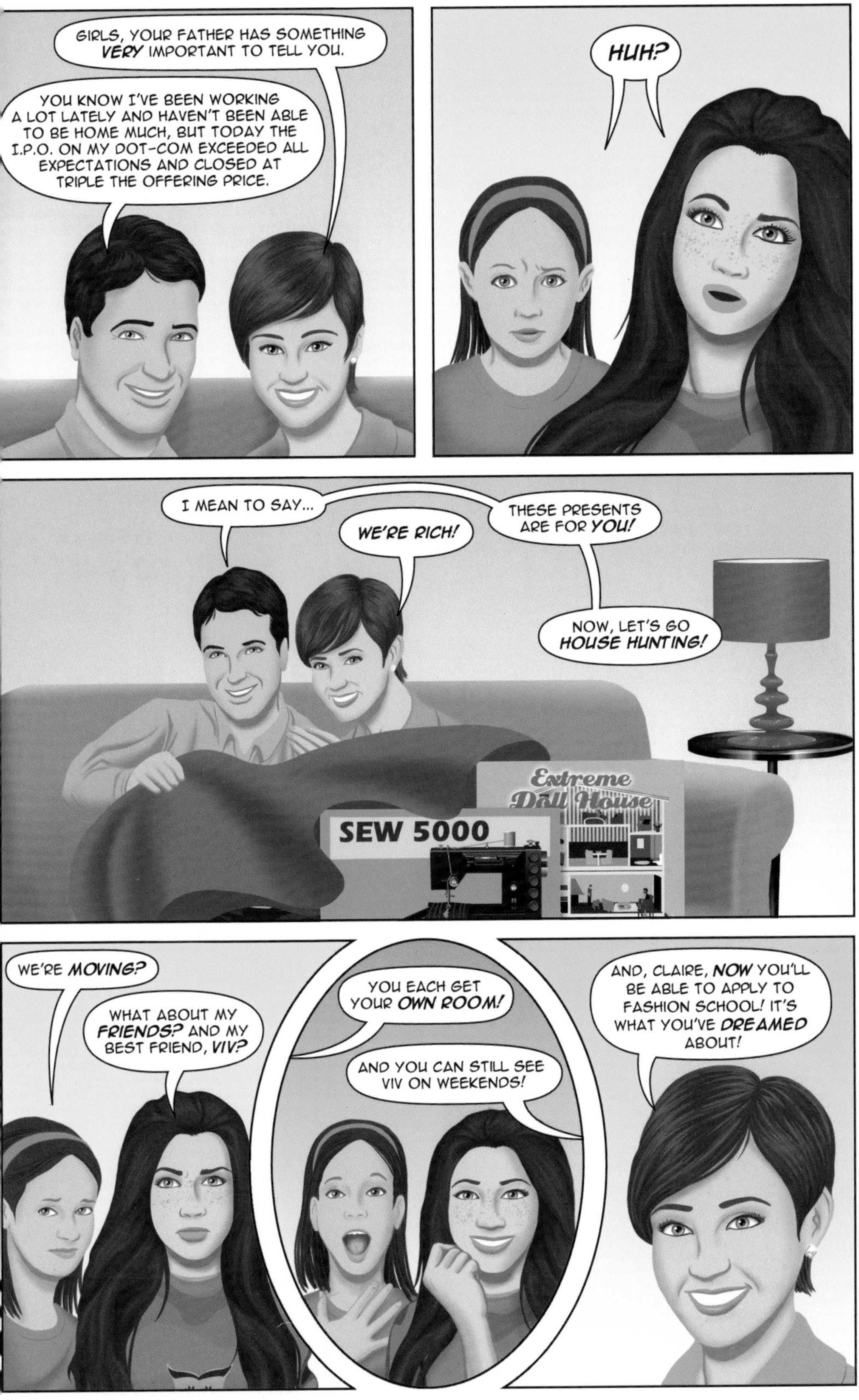
GIRLS, YOUR FATHER HAS SOMETHING VERY IMPORTANT TO TELL YOU.
YOU KNOW I'VE BEEN WORKING A LOT LATELY AND HAVEN'T BEEN ABLE TO BE HOME MUCH, BUT TODAY THE I.P.O. ON MY DOT-COM EXCEEDED ALL EXPECTATIONS AND CLOSED AT TRIPLE THE OFFERING PRICE.
HUH?
I MEAN TO SAY...
WE'RE RICH!
THESE PRESENTS ARE FOR YOU!
NOW, LET'S GO HOUSE HUNTING!
Extreme Doll House
SEW 5000
WE'RE MOVING?
WHAT ABOUT MY FRIENDS? AND MY BEST FRIEND, VIV?
YOU EACH GET YOUR OWN ROOM!
AND YOU CAN STILL SEE VIV ON WEEKENDS!
AND, CLAIRE, NOW YOU'LL BE ABLE TO APPLY TO FASHION SCHOOL! IT'S WHAT YOU'VE DREAMED ABOUT!

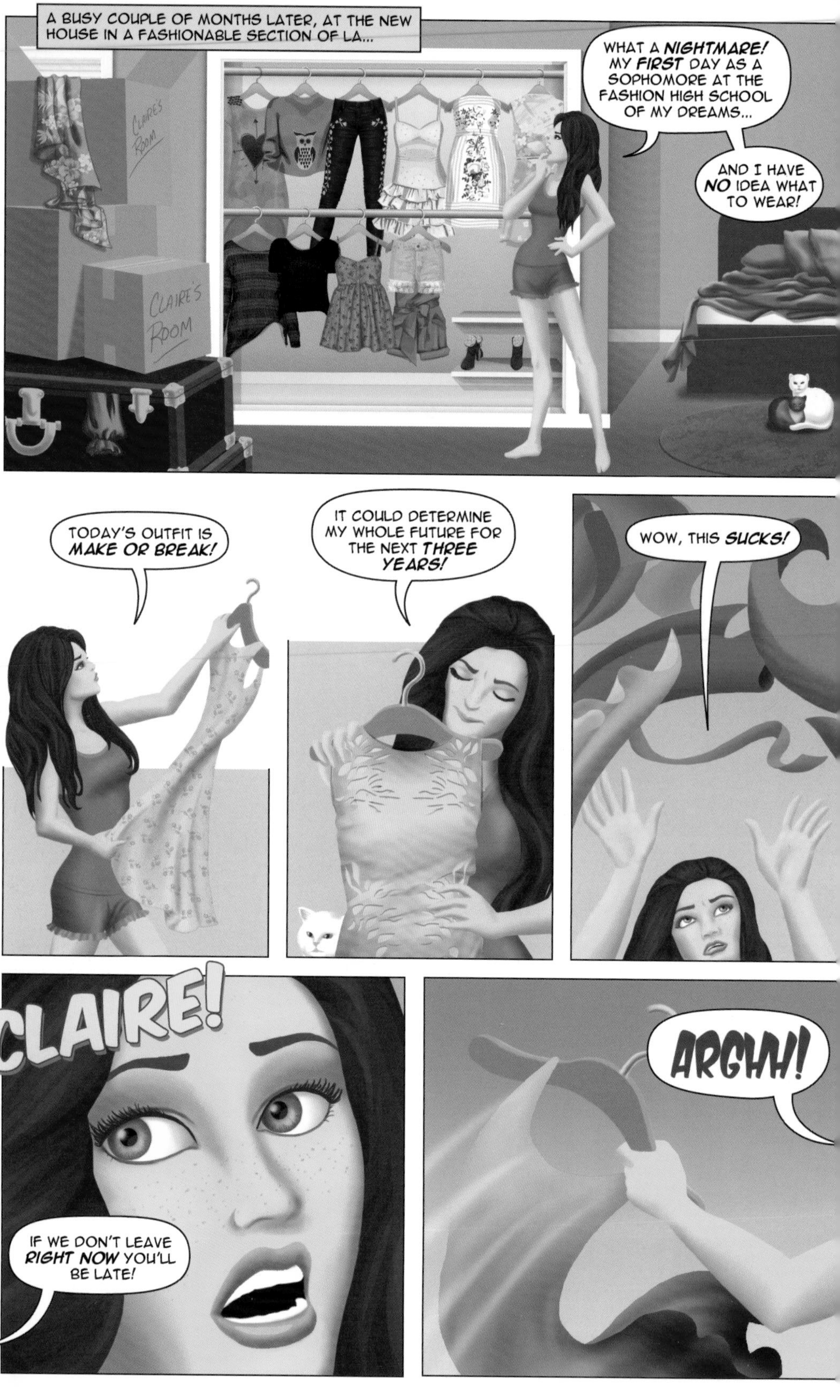
A BUSY COUPLE OF MONTHS LATER, AT THE NEW HOUSE IN A FASHIONABLE SECTION OF LA...
WHAT A NIGHTMARE! MY FIRST DAY AS A SOPHOMORE AT THE FASHION HIGH SCHOOL OF MY DREAMS...
AND I HAVE NO IDEA WHAT TO WEAR!
CLAIRE'S ROOM
CLAIRE'S ROOM
TODAY'S OUTFIT IS MAKE OR BREAK!
IT COULD DETERMINE MY WHOLE FUTURE FOR THE NEXT THREE YEARS!
WOW, THIS SUCKS!
CLAIRE!
IF WE DON'T LEAVE RIGHT NOW YOU'LL BE LATE!
ARGHH!

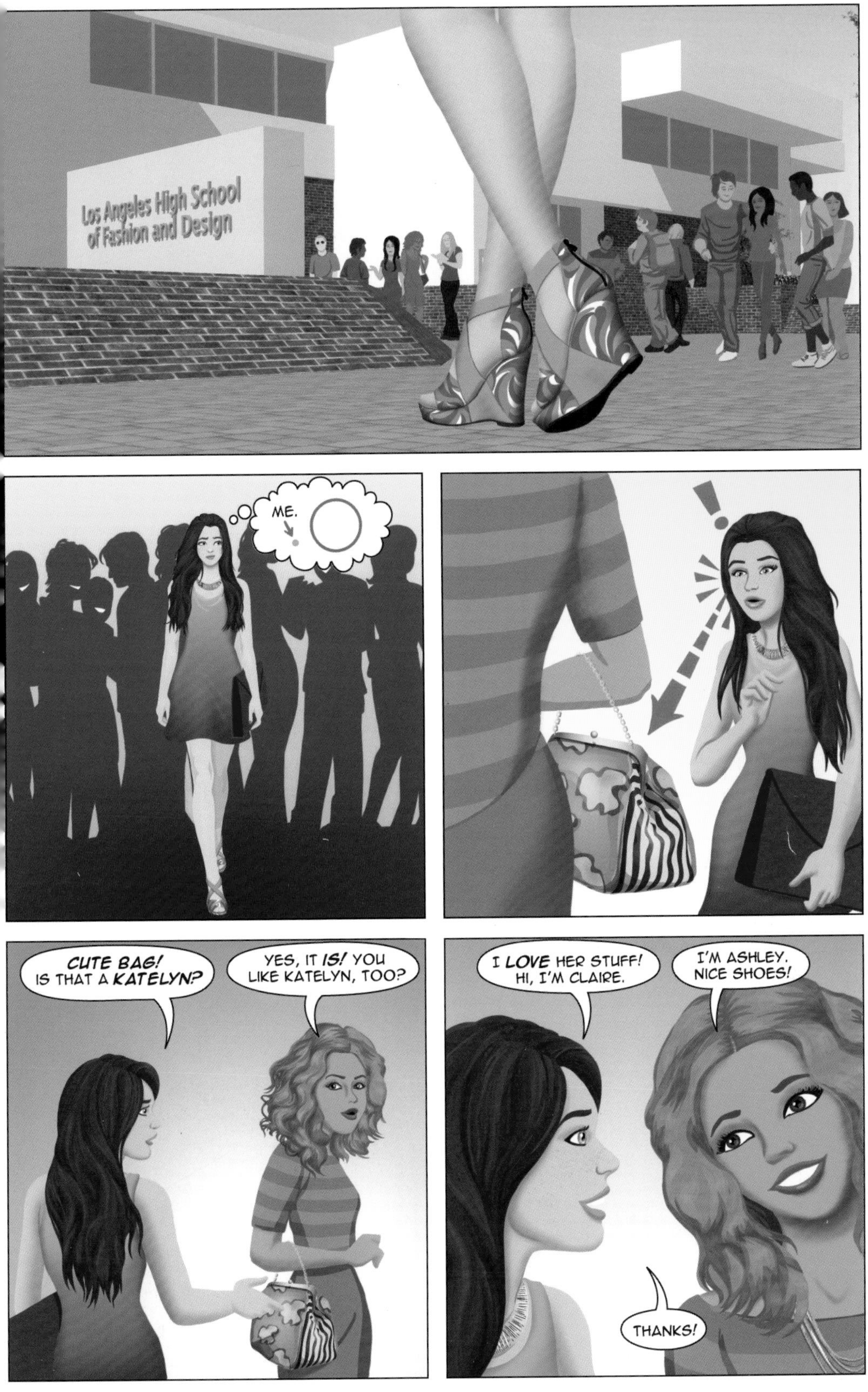
Los Angeles High School of Fashion and Design
ME.
CUTE BAG! IS THAT A KATELYN?
YES, IT IS! YOU LIKE KATELYN, TOO?
I LOVE HER STUFF! HI, I'M CLAIRE.
I'M ASHLEY. NICE SHOES!
THANKS!

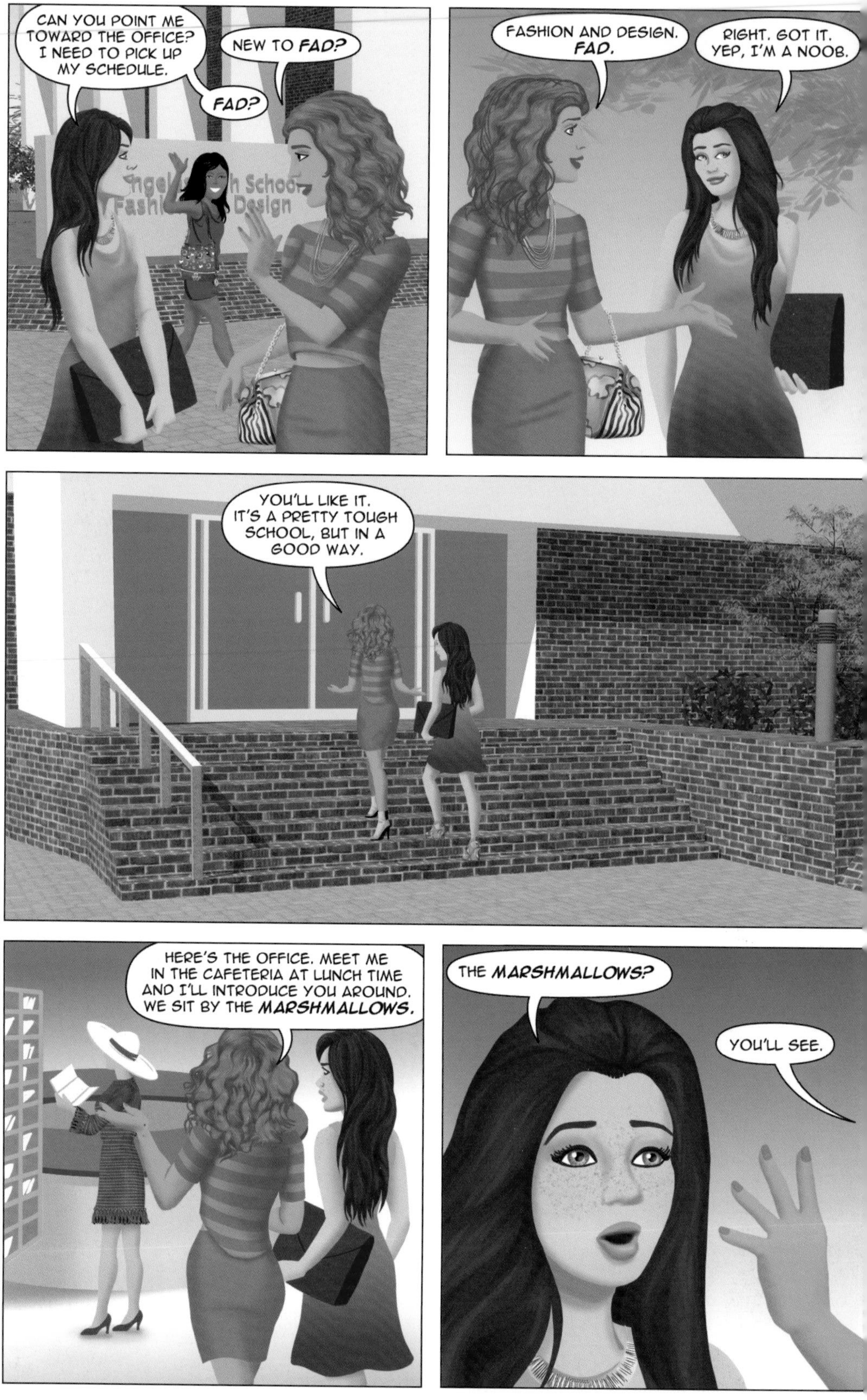
CAN YOU POINT ME TOWARD THE OFFICE? I NEED TO PICK UP MY SCHEDULE.
NEW TO *FAD?*
FAD?
FASHION AND DESIGN. *FAD.*
RIGHT. GOT IT. YEP, I'M A NOOB.
YOU'LL LIKE IT. IT'S A PRETTY TOUGH SCHOOL, BUT IN A GOOD WAY.
HERE'S THE OFFICE. MEET ME IN THE CAFETERIA AT LUNCH TIME AND I'LL INTRODUCE YOU AROUND. WE SIT BY THE *MARSHMALLOWS.*
THE *MARSHMALLOWS?*
YOU'LL SEE.

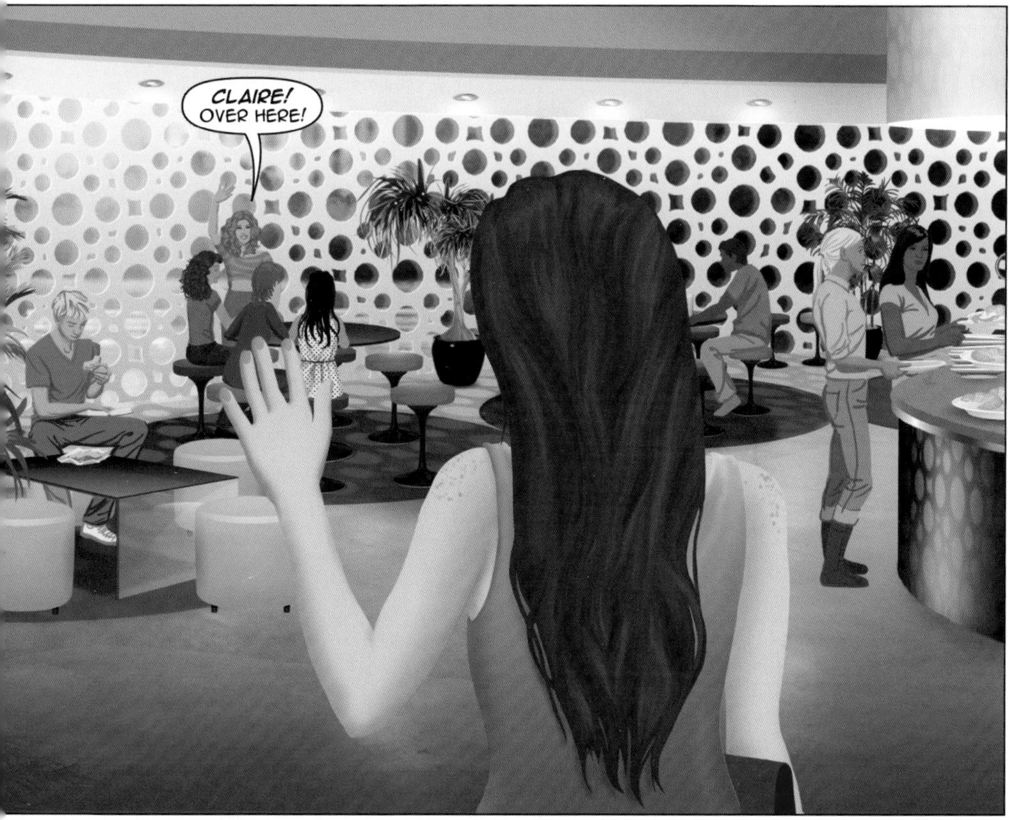
CLAIRE! OVER HERE!

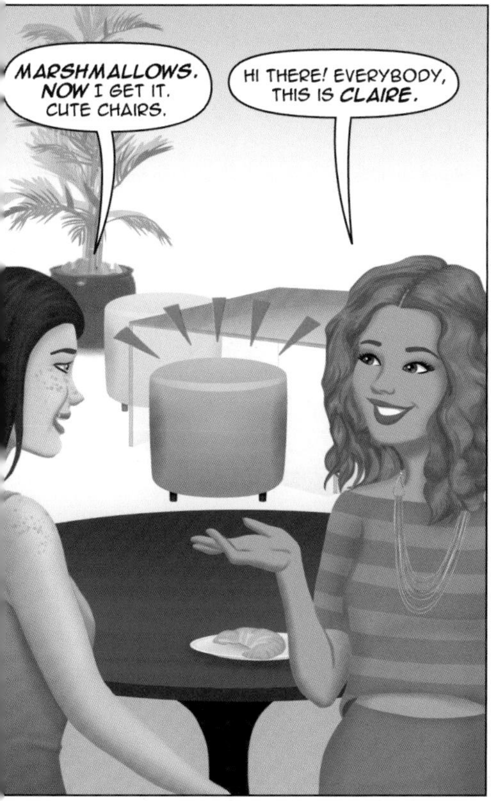
MARSHMALLOWS. NOW I GET IT. CUTE CHAIRS.
HI THERE! EVERYBODY, THIS IS CLAIRE.

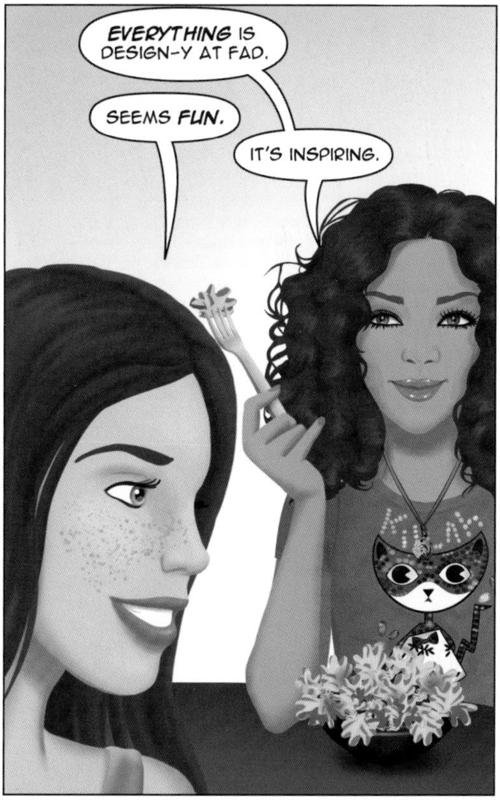
EVERYTHING IS DESIGN-Y AT FAD.
SEEMS FUN.
IT'S INSPIRING.

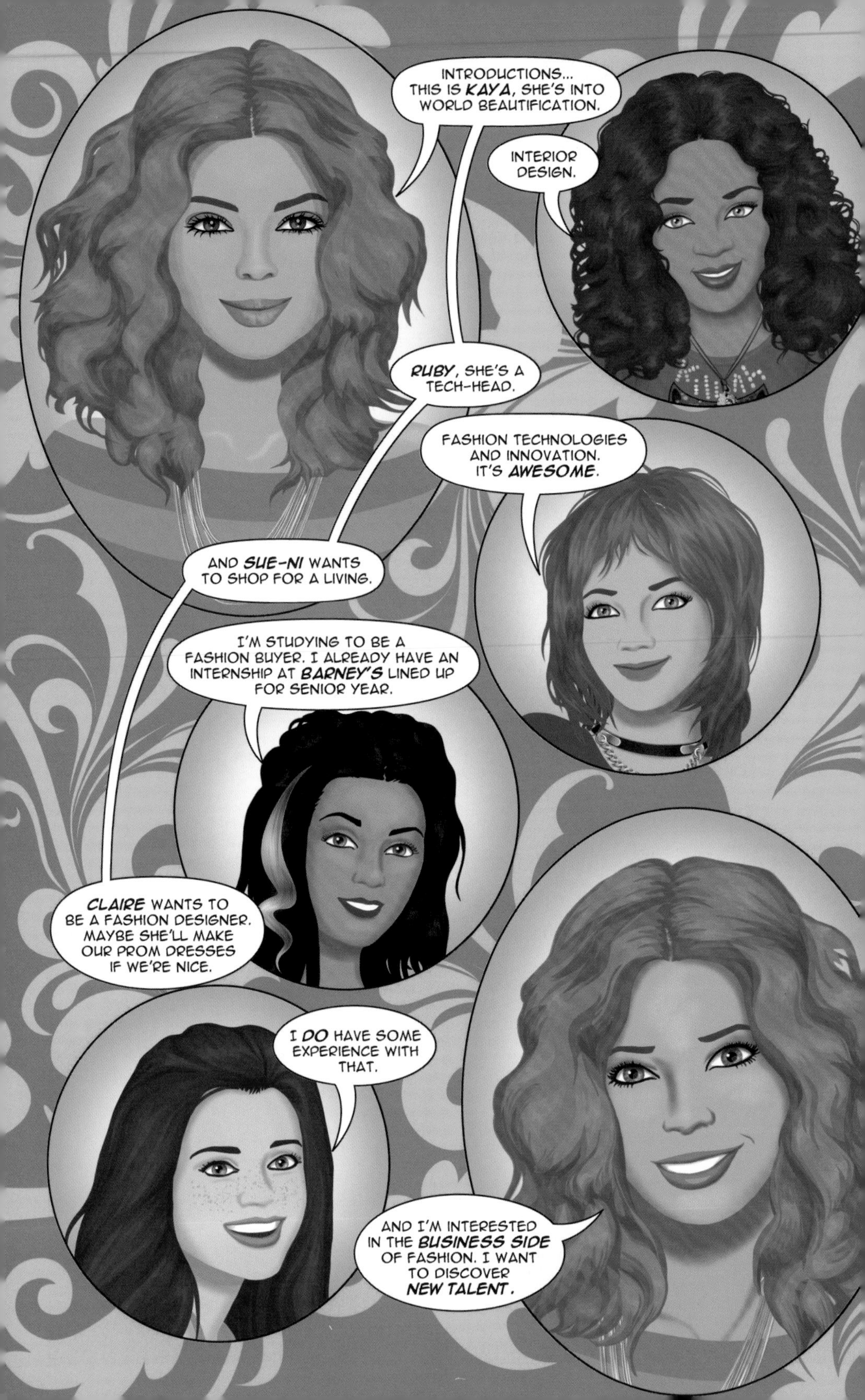
INTRODUCTIONS... THIS IS *KAYA*, SHE'S INTO WORLD BEAUTIFICATION.
INTERIOR DESIGN.
RUBY, SHE'S A TECH-HEAD.
FASHION TECHNOLOGIES AND INNOVATION. IT'S *AWESOME*.
AND *SUE-NI* WANTS TO SHOP FOR A LIVING.
I'M STUDYING TO BE A FASHION BUYER. I ALREADY HAVE AN INTERNSHIP AT *BARNEY'S* LINED UP FOR SENIOR YEAR.
CLAIRE WANTS TO BE A FASHION DESIGNER. MAYBE SHE'LL MAKE OUR PROM DRESSES IF WE'RE NICE.
I *DO* HAVE SOME EXPERIENCE WITH THAT.
AND I'M INTERESTED IN THE *BUSINESS SIDE* OF FASHION. I WANT TO DISCOVER *NEW TALENT*.

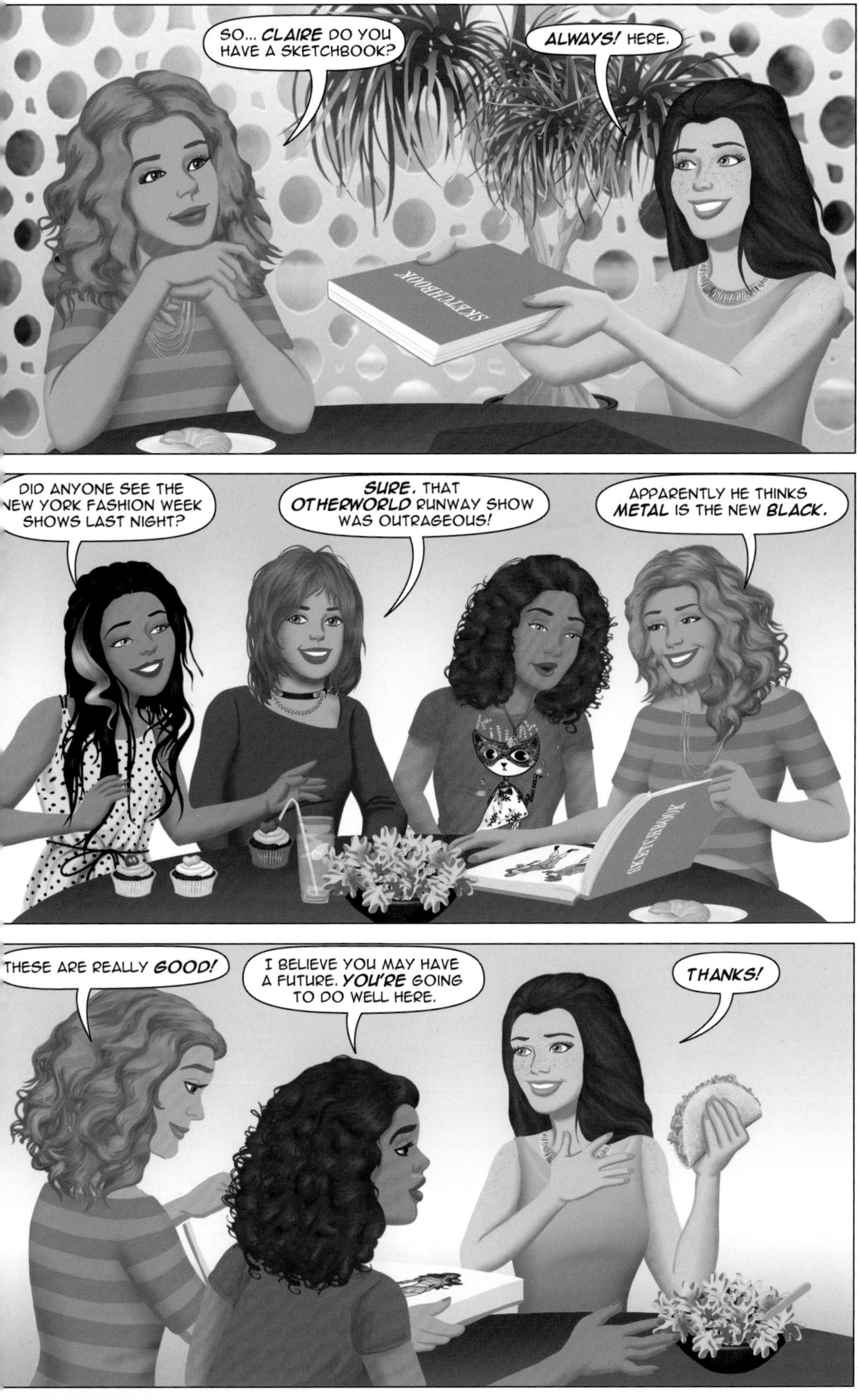

SO... CLAIRE DO YOU HAVE A SKETCHBOOK?
ALWAYS! HERE.
DID ANYONE SEE THE EW YORK FASHION WEEK SHOWS LAST NIGHT?
SURE. THAT OTHERWORLD RUNWAY SHOW WAS OUTRAGEOUS!
APPARENTLY HE THINKS METAL IS THE NEW BLACK.
THESE ARE REALLY GOOD!
I BELIEVE YOU MAY HAVE A FUTURE. YOU'RE GOING TO DO WELL HERE.
THANKS!

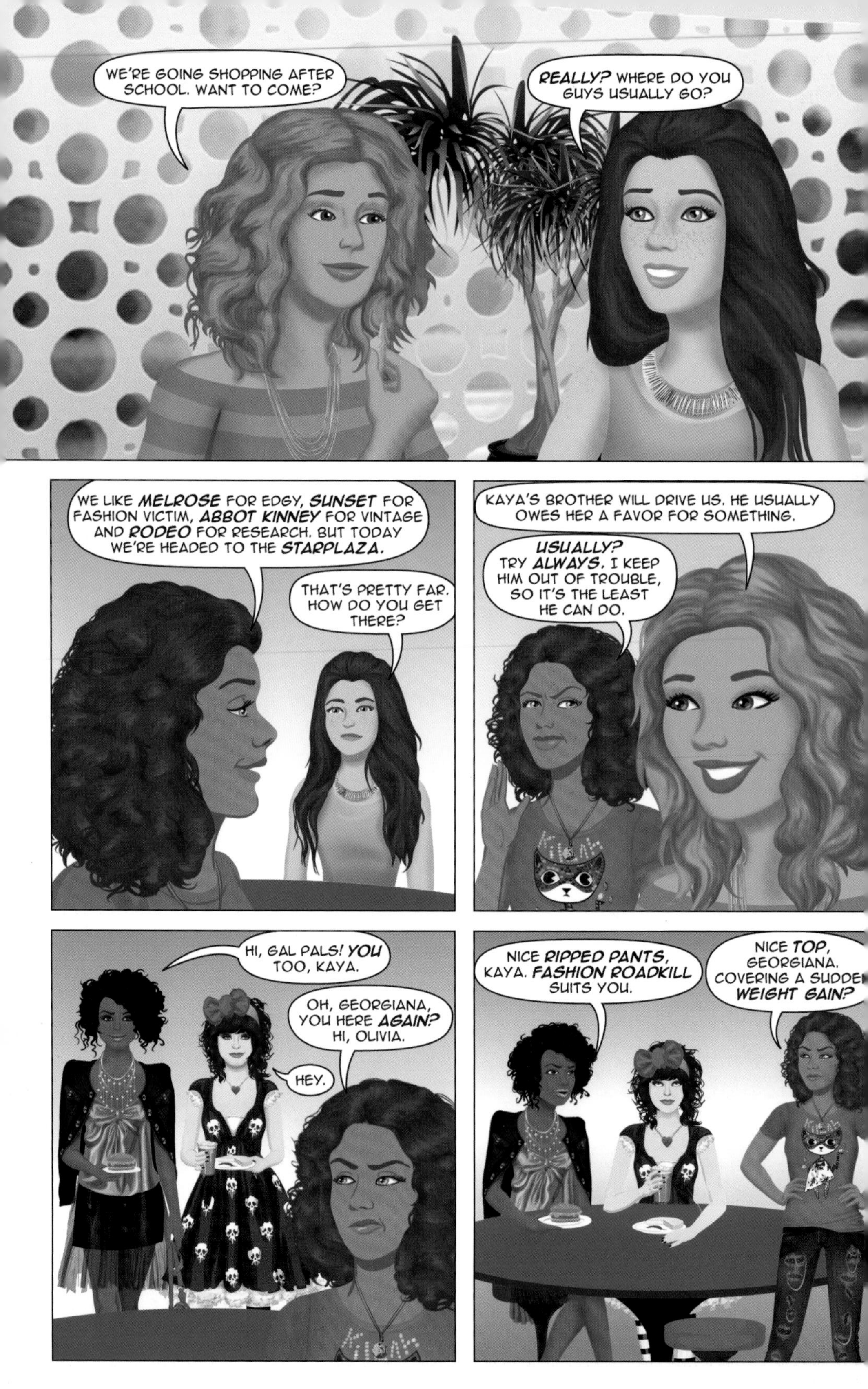
WE'RE GOING SHOPPING AFTER SCHOOL. WANT TO COME?
REALLY? WHERE DO YOU GUYS USUALLY GO?
WE LIKE MELROSE FOR EDGY, SUNSET FOR FASHION VICTIM, ABBOT KINNEY FOR VINTAGE AND RODEO FOR RESEARCH. BUT TODAY WE'RE HEADED TO THE STARPLAZA.
THAT'S PRETTY FAR. HOW DO YOU GET THERE?
KAYA'S BROTHER WILL DRIVE US. HE USUALLY OWES HER A FAVOR FOR SOMETHING.
USUALLY? TRY ALWAYS. I KEEP HIM OUT OF TROUBLE, SO IT'S THE LEAST HE CAN DO.
HI, GAL PALS! YOU TOO, KAYA.
OH, GEORGIANA, YOU HERE AGAIN? HI, OLIVIA.
HEY.
NICE RIPPED PANTS, KAYA. FASHION ROADKILL SUITS YOU.
NICE TOP, GEORGIANA. COVERING A SUDDE WEIGHT GAIN?

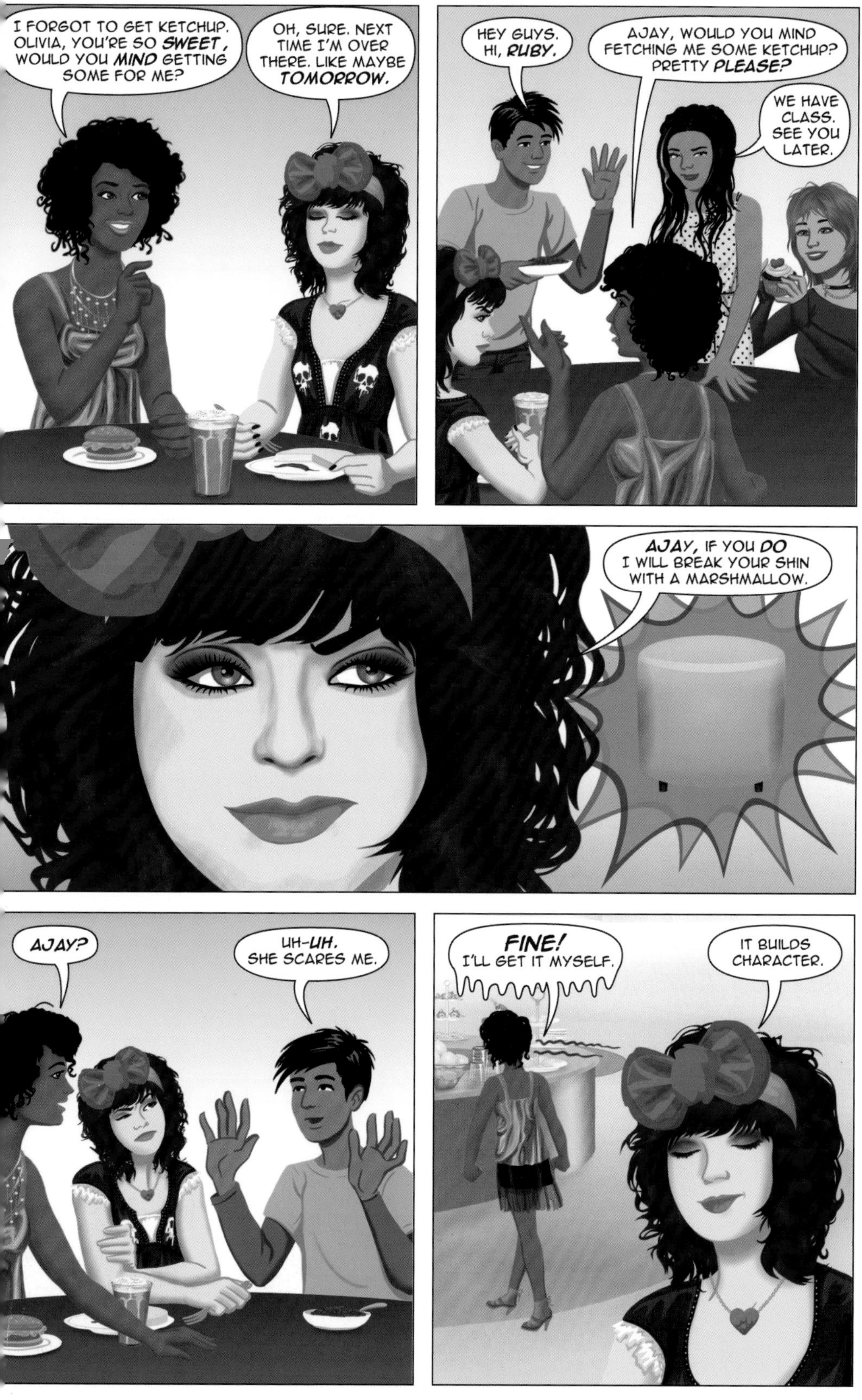
I FORGOT TO GET KETCHUP. OLIVIA, YOU'RE SO *SWEET*, WOULD YOU *MIND* GETTING SOME FOR ME?
OH, SURE. NEXT TIME I'M OVER THERE. LIKE MAYBE *TOMORROW.*
HEY GUYS. HI, *RUBY.*
AJAY, WOULD YOU MIND FETCHING ME SOME KETCHUP? PRETTY *PLEASE?*
WE HAVE CLASS. SEE YOU LATER.
AJAY, IF YOU *DO* I WILL BREAK YOUR SHIN WITH A MARSHMALLOW.
AJAY?
UH-*UH.* SHE SCARES ME.
FINE! I'LL GET IT MYSELF.
IT BUILDS CHARACTER.

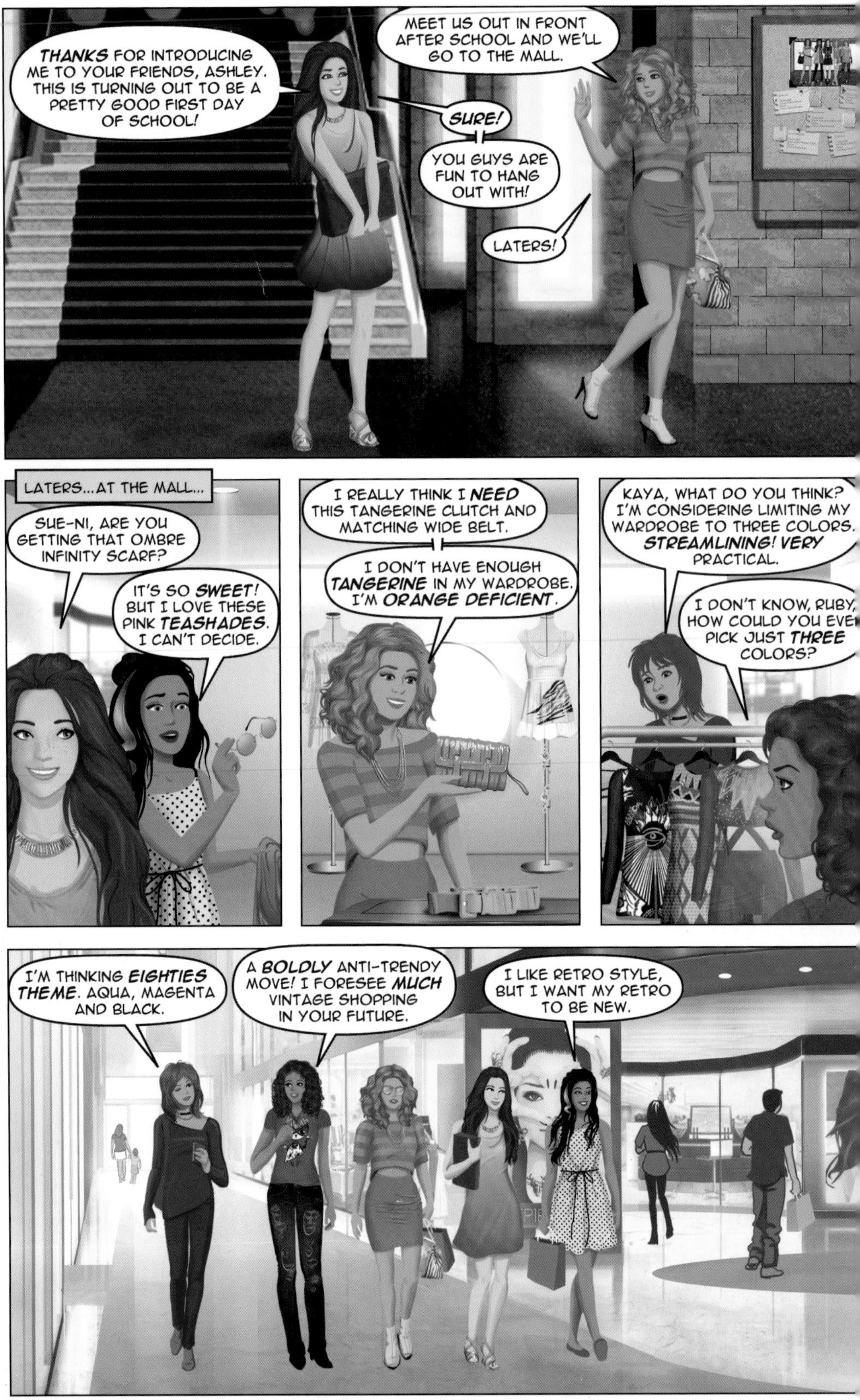

THANKS FOR INTRODUCING ME TO YOUR FRIENDS, ASHLEY. THIS IS TURNING OUT TO BE A PRETTY GOOD FIRST DAY OF SCHOOL!
MEET US OUT IN FRONT AFTER SCHOOL AND WE'LL GO TO THE MALL.
SURE!
YOU GUYS ARE FUN TO HANG OUT WITH!
LATERS!
LATERS...AT THE MALL...
SUE-NI, ARE YOU GETTING THAT OMBRE INFINITY SCARF?
IT'S SO SWEET! BUT I LOVE THESE PINK TEASHADES. I CAN'T DECIDE.
I REALLY THINK I NEED THIS TANGERINE CLUTCH AND MATCHING WIDE BELT.
I DON'T HAVE ENOUGH TANGERINE IN MY WARDROBE. I'M ORANGE DEFICIENT.
KAYA, WHAT DO YOU THINK? I'M CONSIDERING LIMITING MY WARDROBE TO THREE COLORS. STREAMLINING! VERY PRACTICAL.
I DON'T KNOW, RUBY, HOW COULD YOU EVE PICK JUST THREE COLORS?
I'M THINKING EIGHTIES THEME. AQUA, MAGENTA AND BLACK.
A BOLDLY ANTI-TRENDY MOVE! I FORESEE MUCH VINTAGE SHOPPING IN YOUR FUTURE.
I LIKE RETRO STYLE, BUT I WANT MY RETRO TO BE NEW.

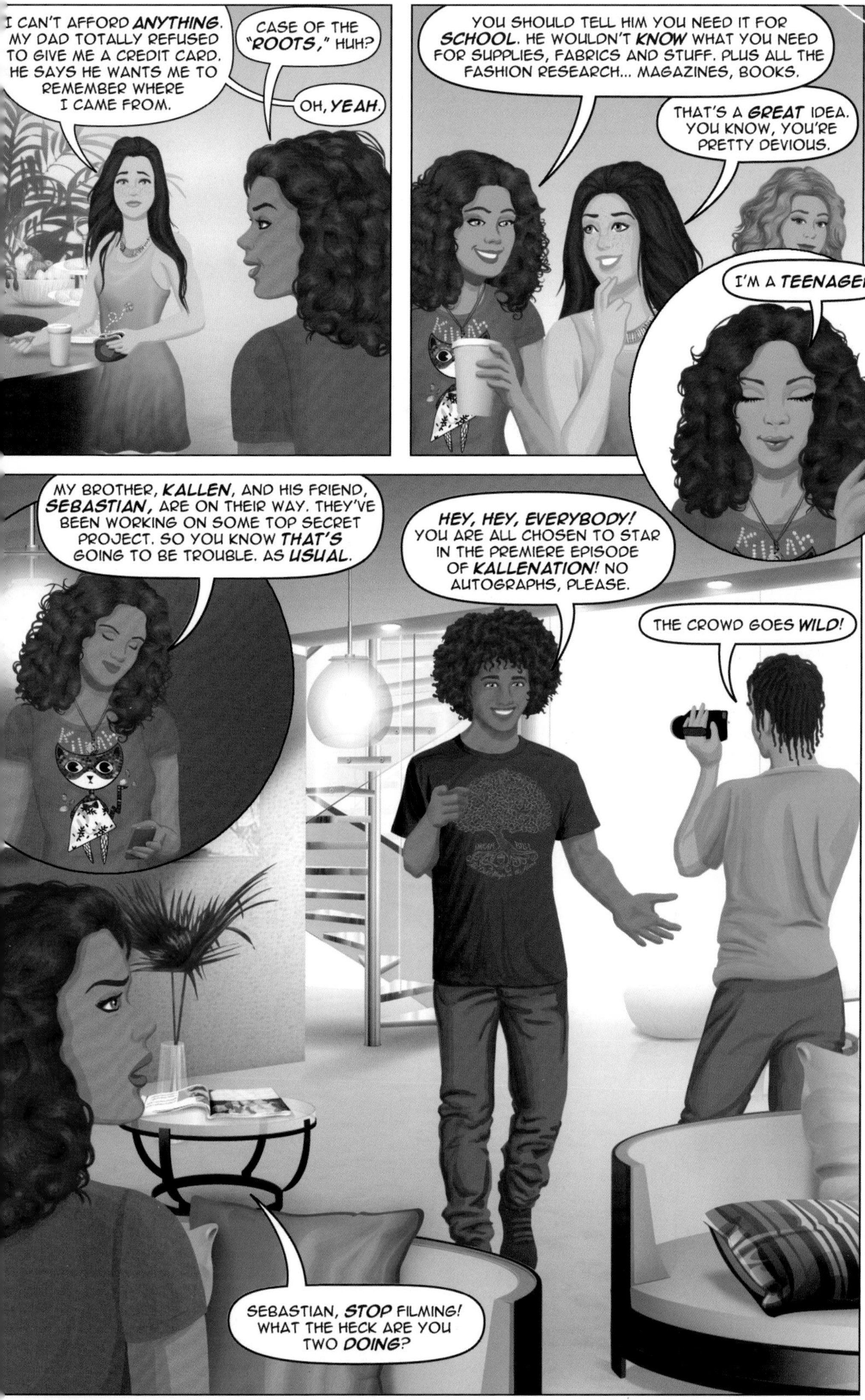
I CAN'T AFFORD ANYTHING. MY DAD TOTALLY REFUSED TO GIVE ME A CREDIT CARD. HE SAYS HE WANTS ME TO REMEMBER WHERE I CAME FROM.
CASE OF THE "ROOTS," HUH?
OH, YEAH.
YOU SHOULD TELL HIM YOU NEED IT FOR SCHOOL. HE WOULDN'T KNOW WHAT YOU NEED FOR SUPPLIES, FABRICS AND STUFF. PLUS ALL THE FASHION RESEARCH... MAGAZINES, BOOKS.
THAT'S A GREAT IDEA. YOU KNOW, YOU'RE PRETTY DEVIOUS.
I'M A TEENAGER.
MY BROTHER, KALLEN, AND HIS FRIEND, SEBASTIAN, ARE ON THEIR WAY. THEY'VE BEEN WORKING ON SOME TOP SECRET PROJECT. SO YOU KNOW THAT'S GOING TO BE TROUBLE. AS USUAL.
HEY, HEY, EVERYBODY! YOU ARE ALL CHOSEN TO STAR IN THE PREMIERE EPISODE OF KALLENATION! NO AUTOGRAPHS, PLEASE.
THE CROWD GOES WILD!
SEBASTIAN, STOP FILMING! WHAT THE HECK ARE YOU TWO DOING?

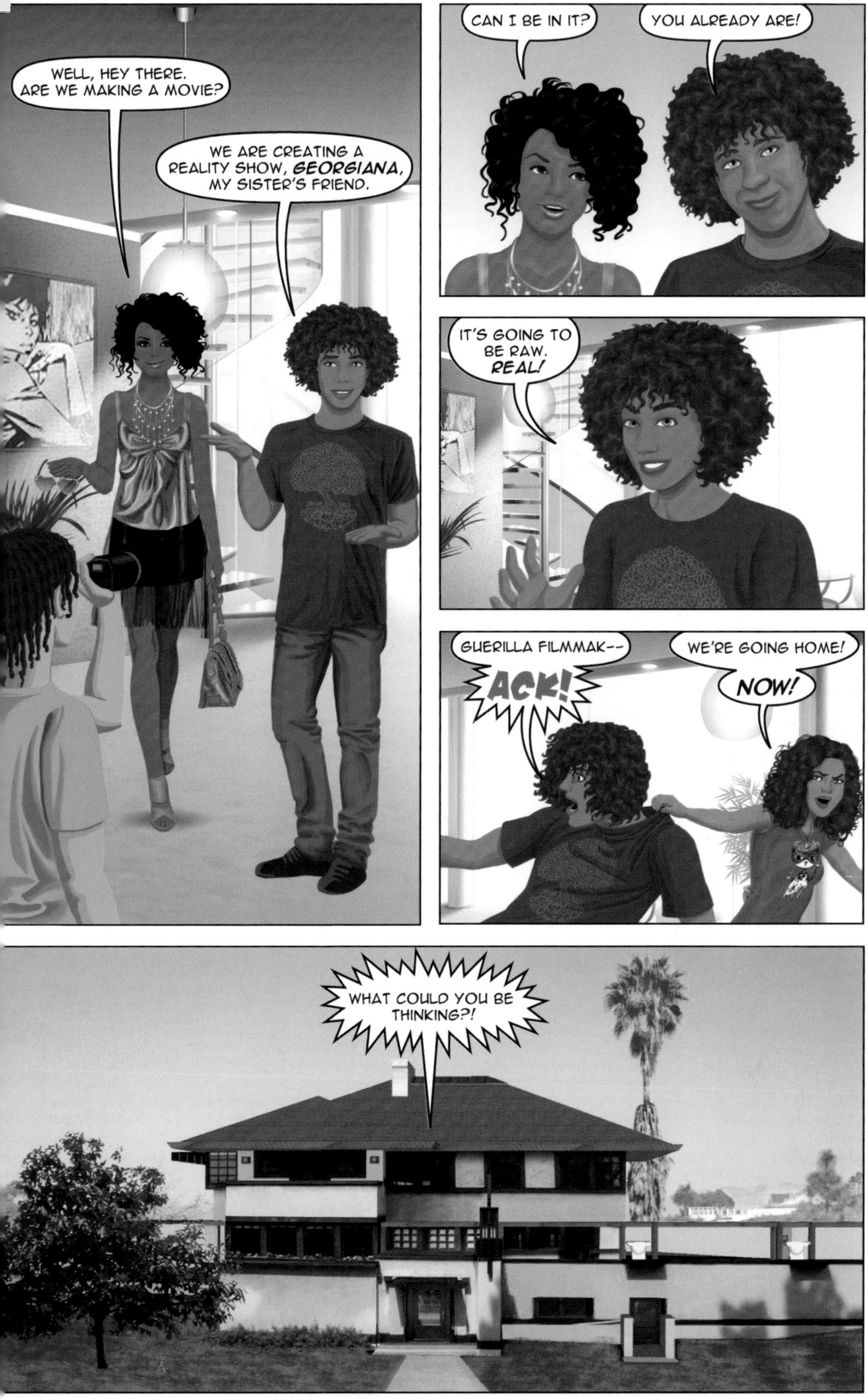
WELL, HEY THERE. ARE WE MAKING A MOVIE?
WE ARE CREATING A REALITY SHOW, GEORGIANA, MY SISTER'S FRIEND.
CAN I BE IN IT?
YOU ALREADY ARE!
IT'S GOING TO BE RAW. REAL!
GUERILLA FILMMAK--
ACK!
WE'RE GOING HOME!
NOW!
WHAT COULD YOU BE THINKING?!

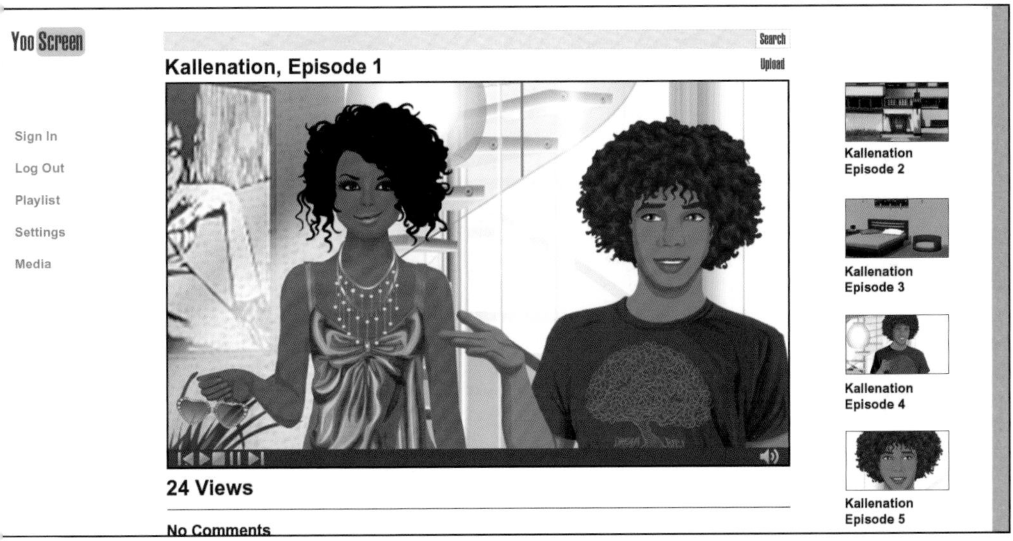
Yoo Screen
Search
Kallenation, Episode 1
Upload
Sign In
Log Out
Playlist
Settings
Media
Kallenation Episode 2
Kallenation Episode 3
Kallenation Episode 4
Kallenation Episode 5
24 Views
No Comments

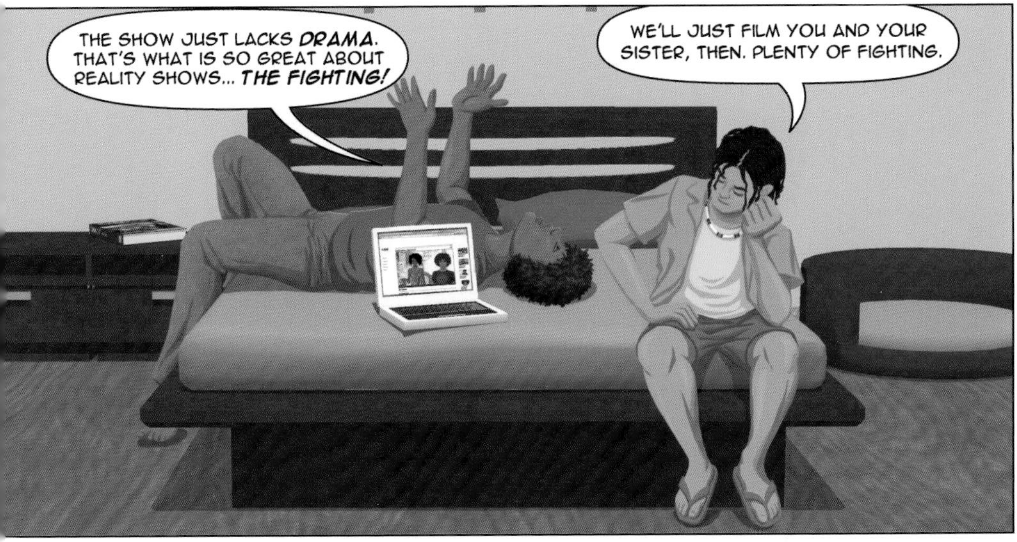
THE SHOW JUST LACKS DRAMA. THAT'S WHAT IS SO GREAT ABOUT REALITY SHOWS... THE FIGHTING!
WE'LL JUST FILM YOU AND YOUR SISTER, THEN. PLENTY OF FIGHTING.

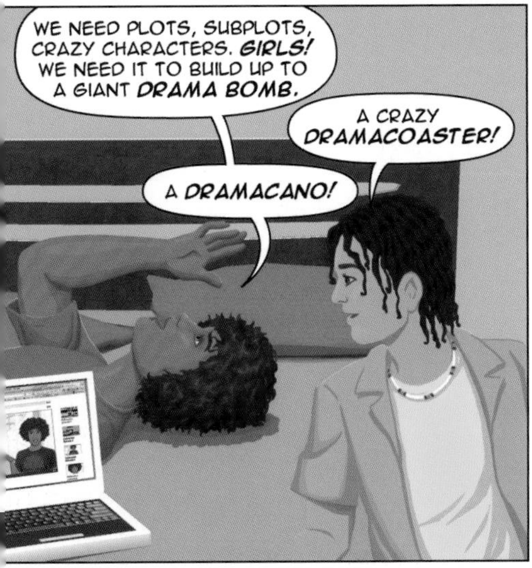
WE NEED PLOTS, SUBPLOTS, CRAZY CHARACTERS. GIRLS! WE NEED IT TO BUILD UP TO A GIANT DRAMA BOMB.
A CRAZY DRAMACOASTER!
A DRAMACANO!

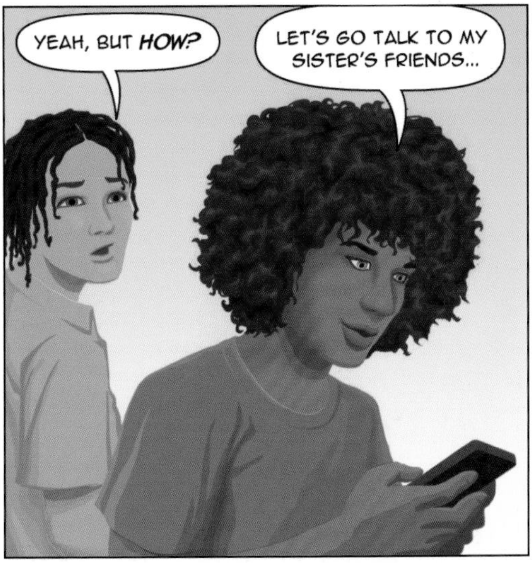
YEAH, BUT HOW?
LET'S GO TALK TO MY SISTER'S FRIENDS...

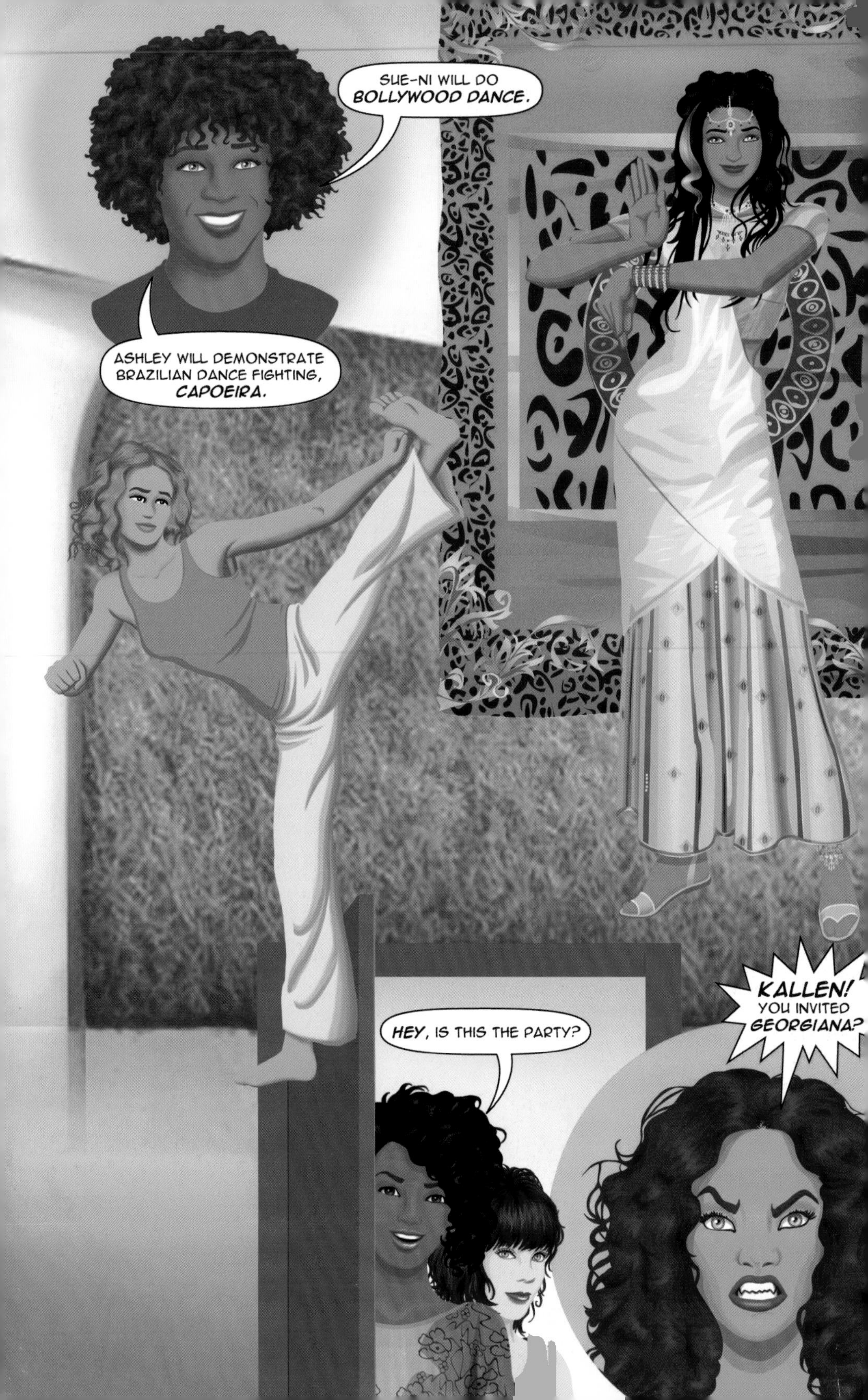
SUE-NI WILL DO BOLLYWOOD DANCE.
ASHLEY WILL DEMONSTRATE BRAZILIAN DANCE FIGHTING, CAPOEIRA.
HEY, IS THIS THE PARTY?
KALLEN! YOU INVITED GEORGIANA?

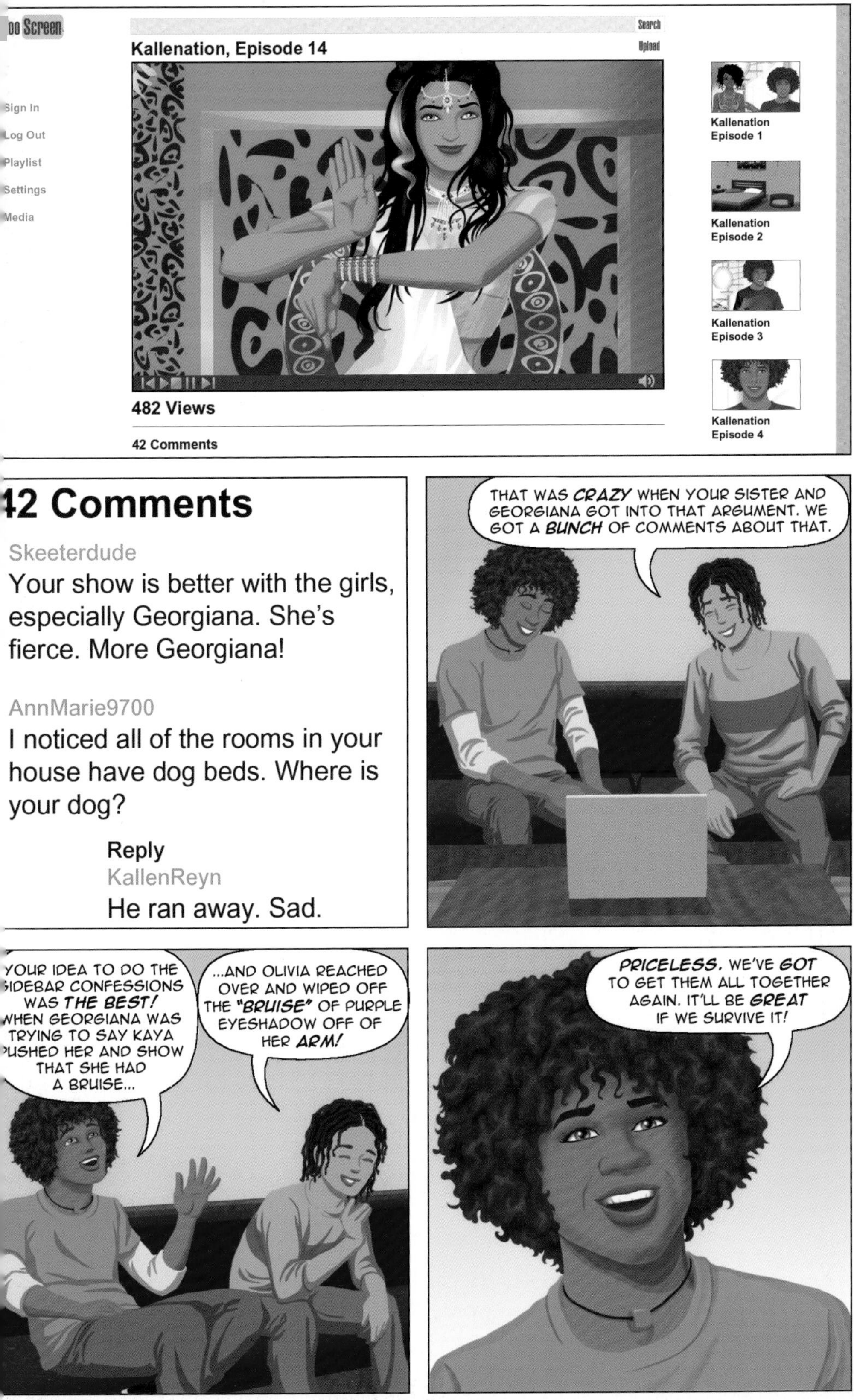
oo Screen
Search
Upload
Kallenation, Episode 14
ign In
og Out
Playlist
Settings
Media
Kallenation Episode 1
Kallenation Episode 2
Kallenation Episode 3
Kallenation Episode 4
482 Views
42 Comments
2 Comments
Skeeterdude
Your show is better with the girls, especially Georgiana. She's fierce. More Georgiana!
AnnMarie9700
I noticed all of the rooms in your house have dog beds. Where is your dog?
Reply
KallenReyn
He ran away. Sad.
THAT WAS CRAZY WHEN YOUR SISTER AND GEORGIANA GOT INTO THAT ARGUMENT. WE GOT A BUNCH OF COMMENTS ABOUT THAT.
YOUR IDEA TO DO THE IDEBAR CONFESSIONS WAS THE BEST! VHEN GEORGIANA WAS TRYING TO SAY KAYA USHED HER AND SHOW THAT SHE HAD A BRUISE...
...AND OLIVIA REACHED OVER AND WIPED OFF THE "BRUISE" OF PURPLE EYESHADOW OFF OF HER ARM!
PRICELESS. WE'VE GOT TO GET THEM ALL TOGETHER AGAIN. IT'LL BE GREAT IF WE SURVIVE IT!

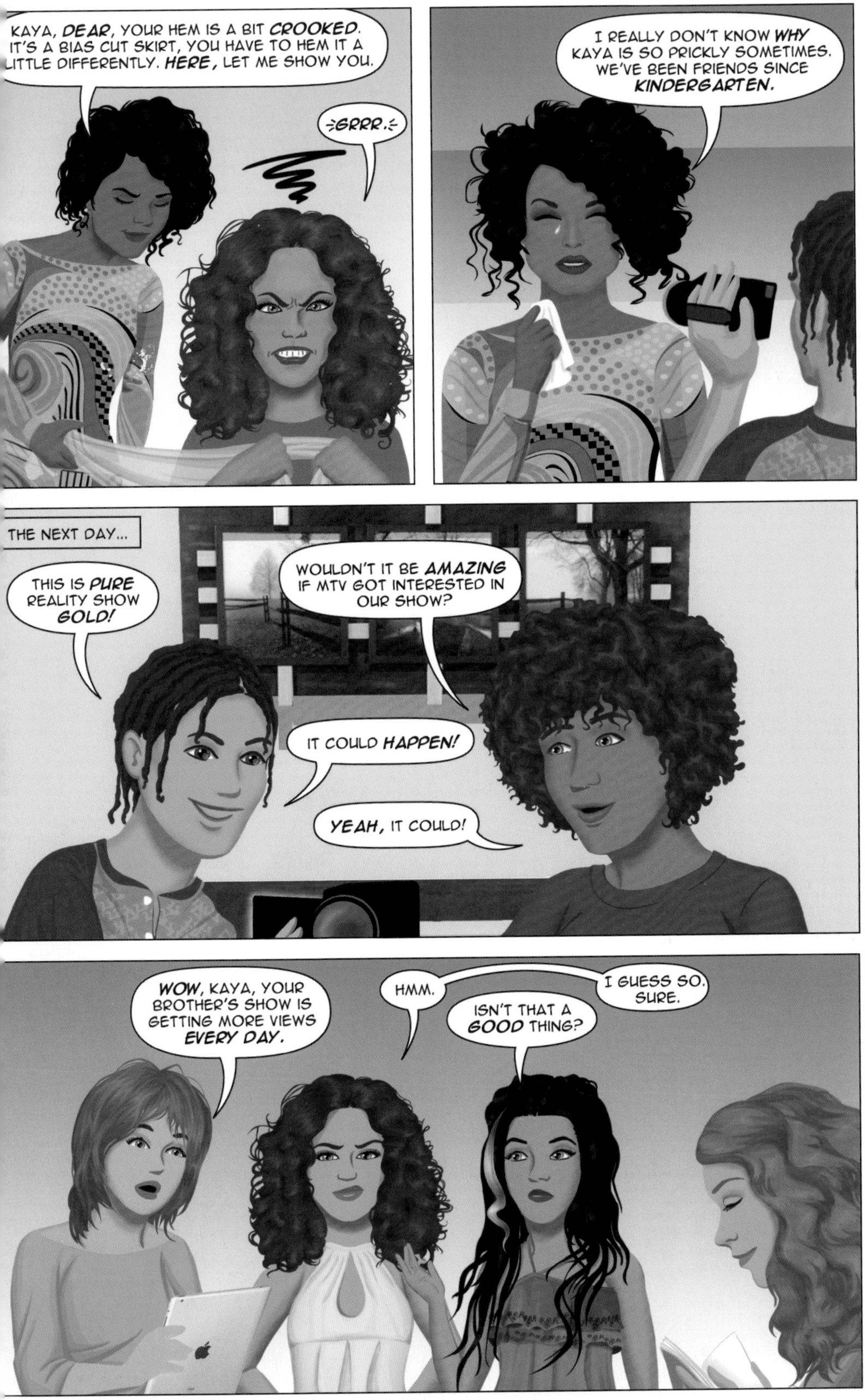

KAYA, DEAR, YOUR HEM IS A BIT CROOKED. IT'S A BIAS CUT SKIRT, YOU HAVE TO HEM IT A LITTLE DIFFERENTLY. HERE, LET ME SHOW YOU.
GRRR.
I REALLY DON'T KNOW WHY KAYA IS SO PRICKLY SOMETIMES. WE'VE BEEN FRIENDS SINCE KINDERGARTEN.
THE NEXT DAY...
THIS IS PURE REALITY SHOW GOLD!
WOULDN'T IT BE AMAZING IF MTV GOT INTERESTED IN OUR SHOW?
IT COULD HAPPEN!
YEAH, IT COULD!
WOW, KAYA, YOUR BROTHER'S SHOW IS GETTING MORE VIEWS EVERY DAY.
HMM.
ISN'T THAT A GOOD THING?
I GUESS SO. SURE.

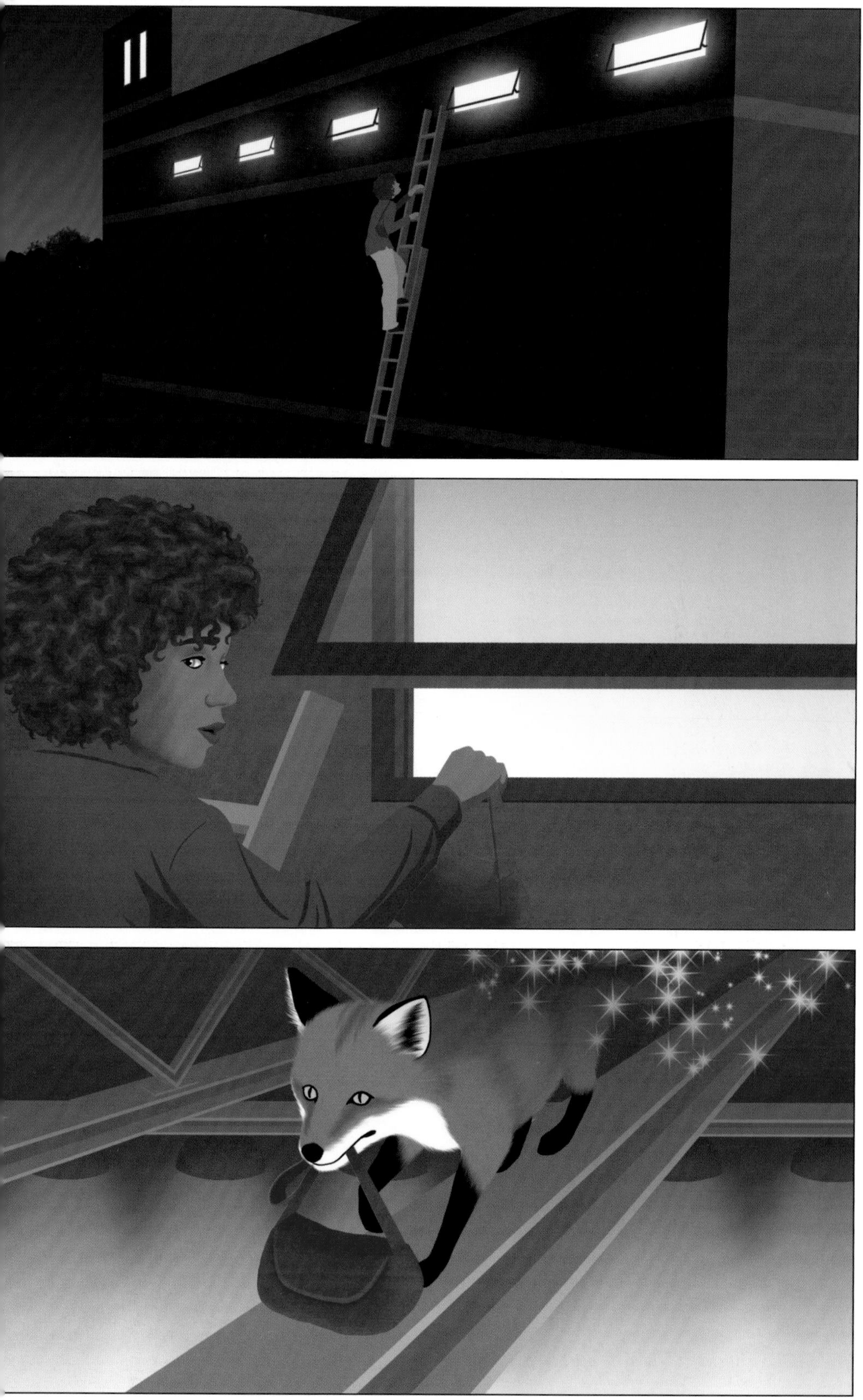

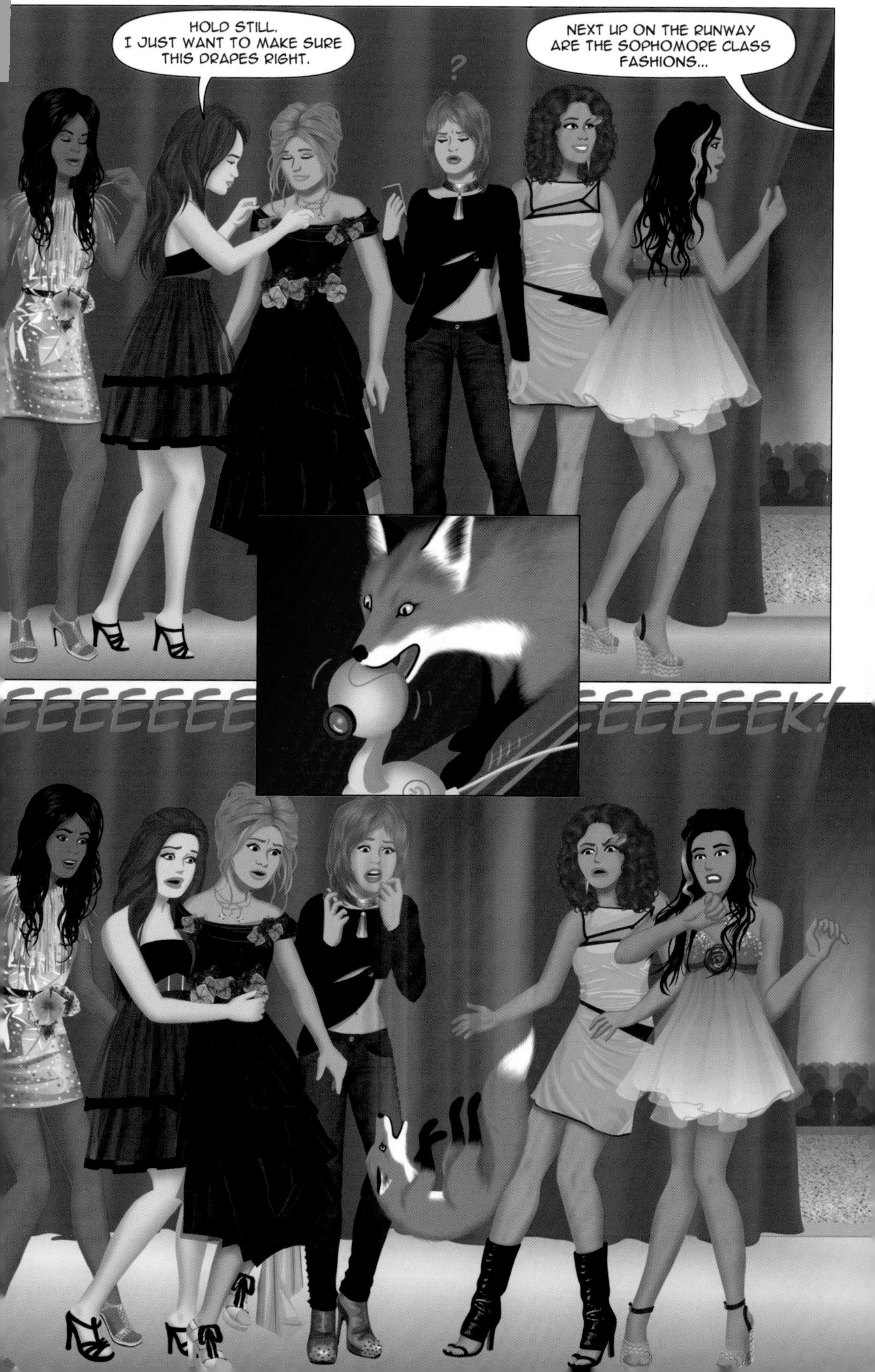
HOLD STILL. I JUST WANT TO MAKE SURE THIS DRAPES RIGHT.
NEXT UP ON THE RUNWAY ARE THE SOPHOMORE CLASS FASHIONS...
?
EEEEEEE
EEEEEEEK!

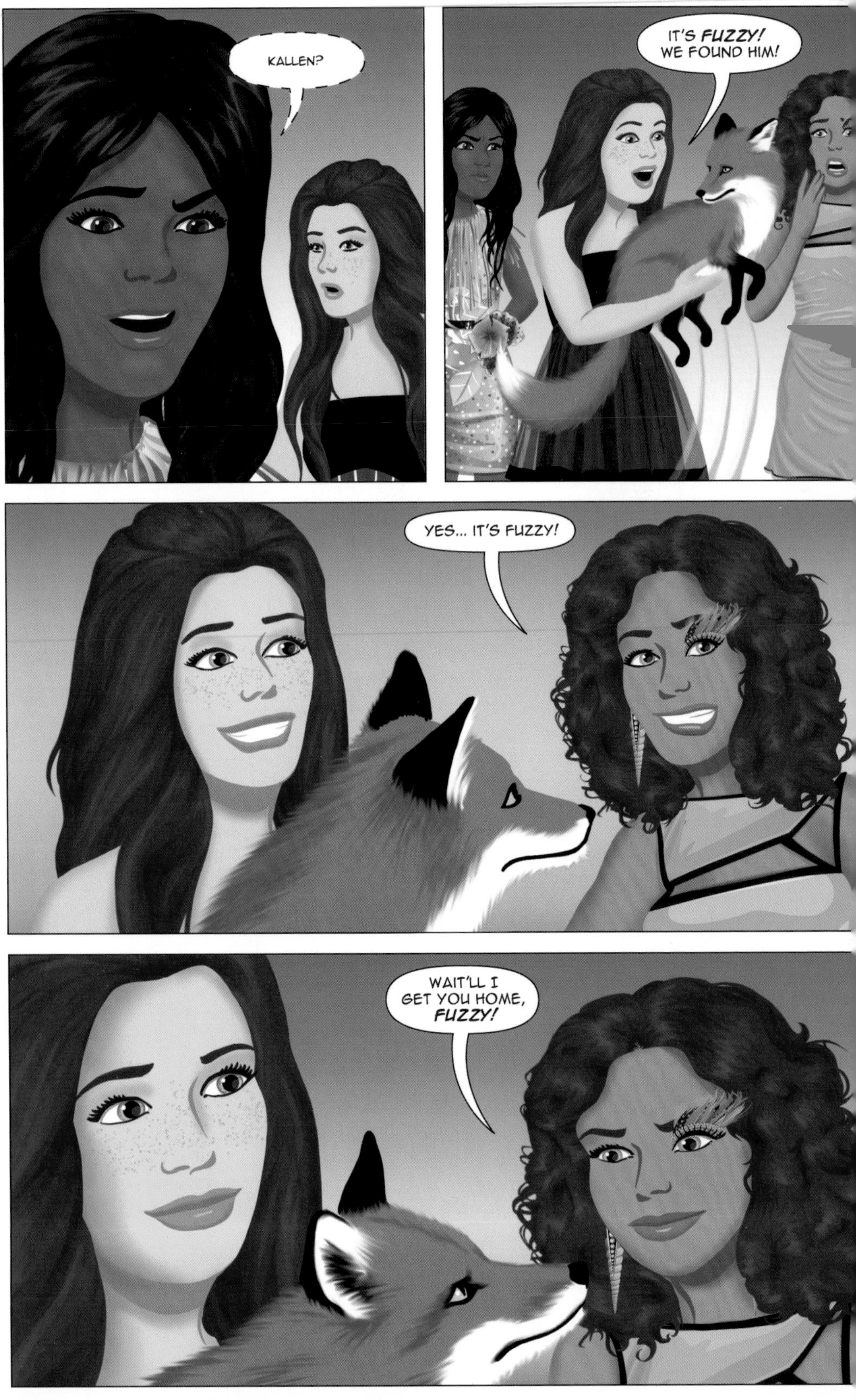
KALLEN?
IT'S FUZZY! WE FOUND HIM!
YES... IT'S FUZZY!
WAIT'LL I GET YOU HOME, FUZZY!

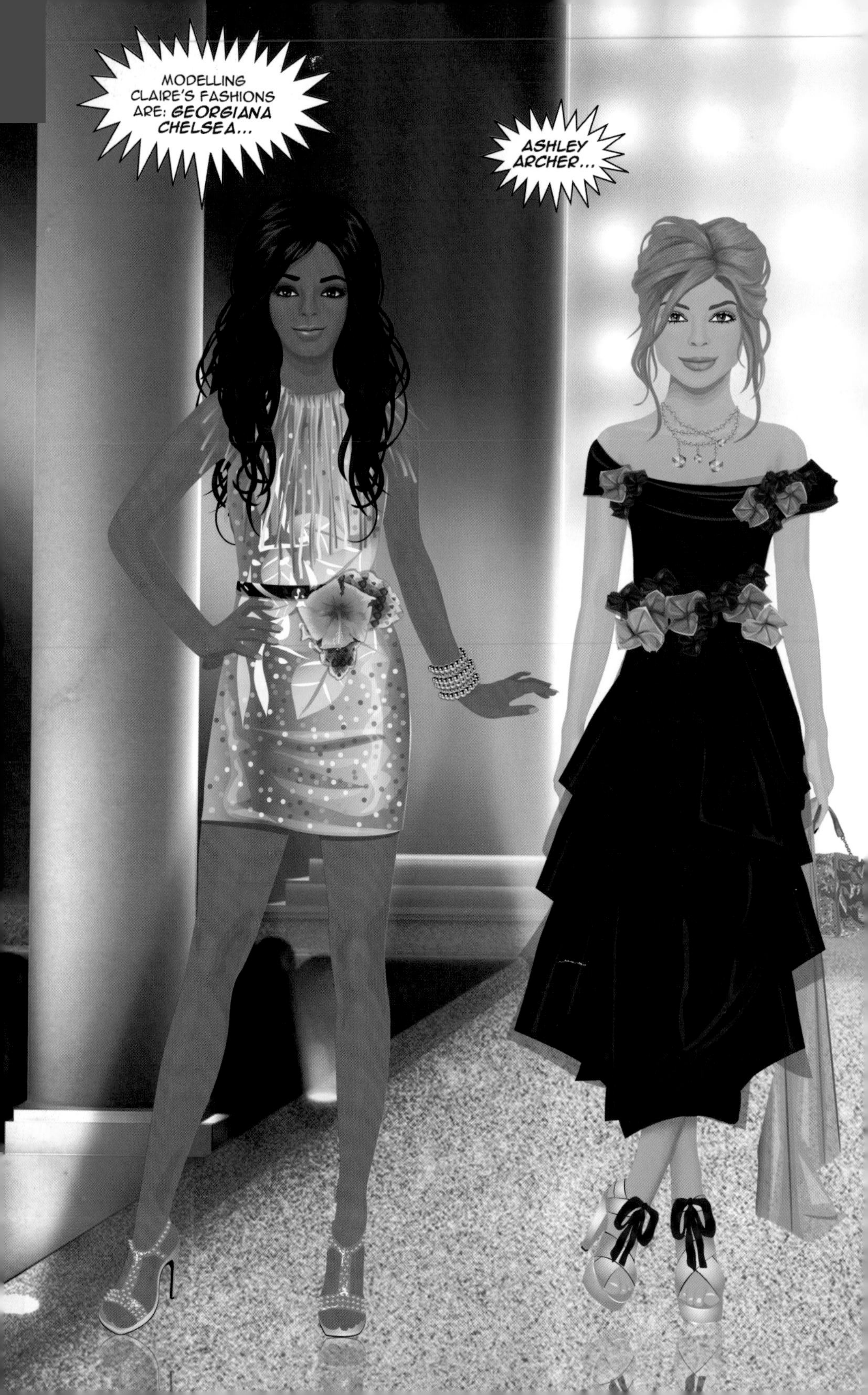
MODELLING CLAIRE'S FASHIONS ARE: GEORGIANA CHELSEA...
ASHLEY ARCHER...

Watch Out For PAPERCUTZ™

Welcome to the fun, fashionable, friend-filled first STARDOLL graphic novel by JayJay Jackson from Papercutz, the fine folks dedicated to publishing great graphic novels for all ages. I'm Editor-in-Chief Jim Salicrup, and I'm here to give you a little bit of background on JayJay Jackson. So I asked her to tell us a little bit about herself:

"I can't remember a time when I didn't want to be an artist. My cousin tells me that at the age of six I was already set on it. Even with precious little encouragement or help in the beginning I obsessively stuck to the path. I became an artist because I HAD to. I've had an eclectic career. I've been an illustrator, graphic designer, art director, painter, writer, editor, web designer, etc. In comics I've worked at Marvel, DC, Valiant, Defiant, Broadway Comics and more.

"The art style in STARDOLL is inspired by the beautiful art on the Stardoll site itself. I've tried to translate that vision into the sequential art form. The emphasis of the book is on fun and fashion with great stories at its heart, so it works for all ages and genders. I think it will surprise people! With STARDOLL I was lucky enough to have an almost blank slate as far as the characters and story goes. Fashion and all other forms of art are my biggest passion in life! The opportunity to do a book with fashion as a central theme is a dream come true. My goal has been to create principle characters who are complex, yearn to reach their goals and have interesting backgrounds and lives and also happen to be female.

"It's been a lot of fun creating the world of STARDOLL and the people in it, based on the rich imagery and fun fashions of the Stardoll site. I'm hooked on the Stardoll site! I go there and play all the time. But not when I'm supposed to be working! I promise!"

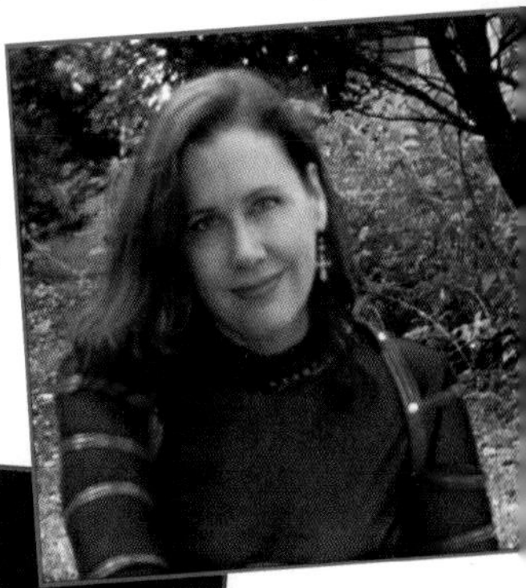

Along with JayJay, we're committed to creating fun, fabulous, and surprise-filled STARDOLL graphic novels. Coming up next, will be STARDOLL #2 "The Secret of the Star Jewel." But in the meantime we also want to introduce you to another fun group of girls—Julie, Lucie, and Alia—who are as passionate about dance, as Ashley, Claire, Kaya, Ruby, and Sue-Ni are about fashion. They all star in another Papercutz graphic novel series, DANCE CLASS by Beka and Crip, and on the following pages we present a sneak peek at DANCE CLASS #6 "A Merry Olde Christmas." Whether you enjoy STARDOLL, DANCE CLASS, or any of the many other Papercutz graphic novels available to you, we want you to know that we want to hear from you. Tell us what you love or what let you down. We want to know what you think, because ultimately we're doing it all for you!

Thanks,
Jim

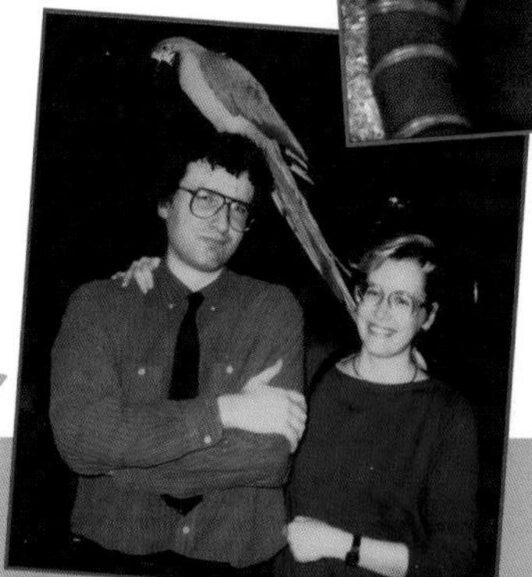

JIM & JAYJAY, A FEW YEARS AGO!

STAY IN TOUCH!

EMAIL: salicrup@papercutz.com
WEB: www.papercutz.com
TWITTER: @papercutzgn
FACEBOOK: PAPERCUTZGRAPHICNOVELS
SNAIL MAIL: Papercutz, 160 Broadway, Suite 700, East Wing, New York, NY 10038

SPECIAL PREVIEW OF DANCE CLASS #6
"A MERRY OLDE CHRISTMAS"

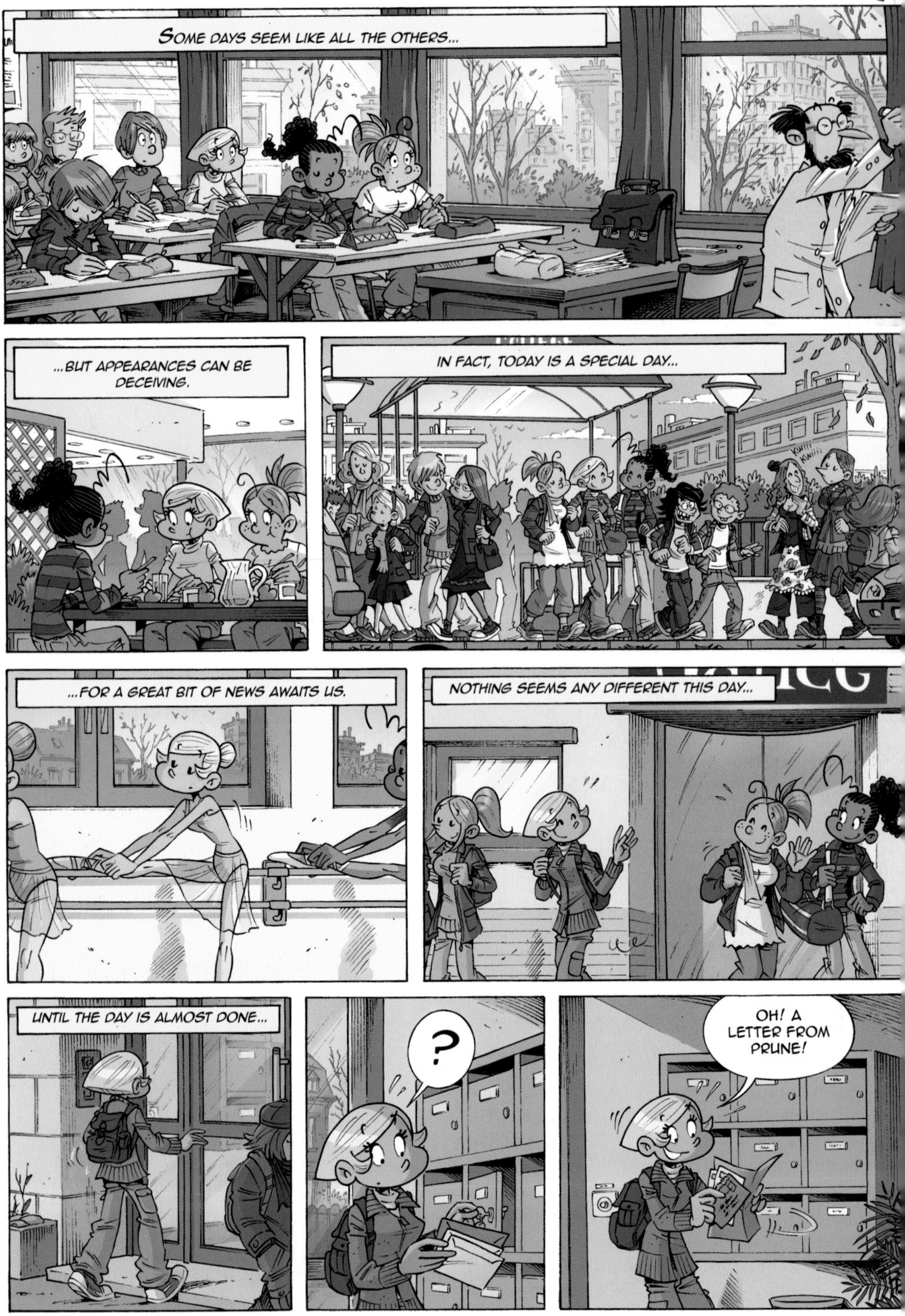

SOME DAYS SEEM LIKE ALL THE OTHERS...
...BUT APPEARANCES CAN BE DECEIVING.
IN FACT, TODAY IS A SPECIAL DAY...
...FOR A GREAT BIT OF NEWS AWAITS US.
NOTHING SEEMS ANY DIFFERENT THIS DAY...
UNTIL THE DAY IS ALMOST DONE...
?
OH! A LETTER FROM PRUNE!

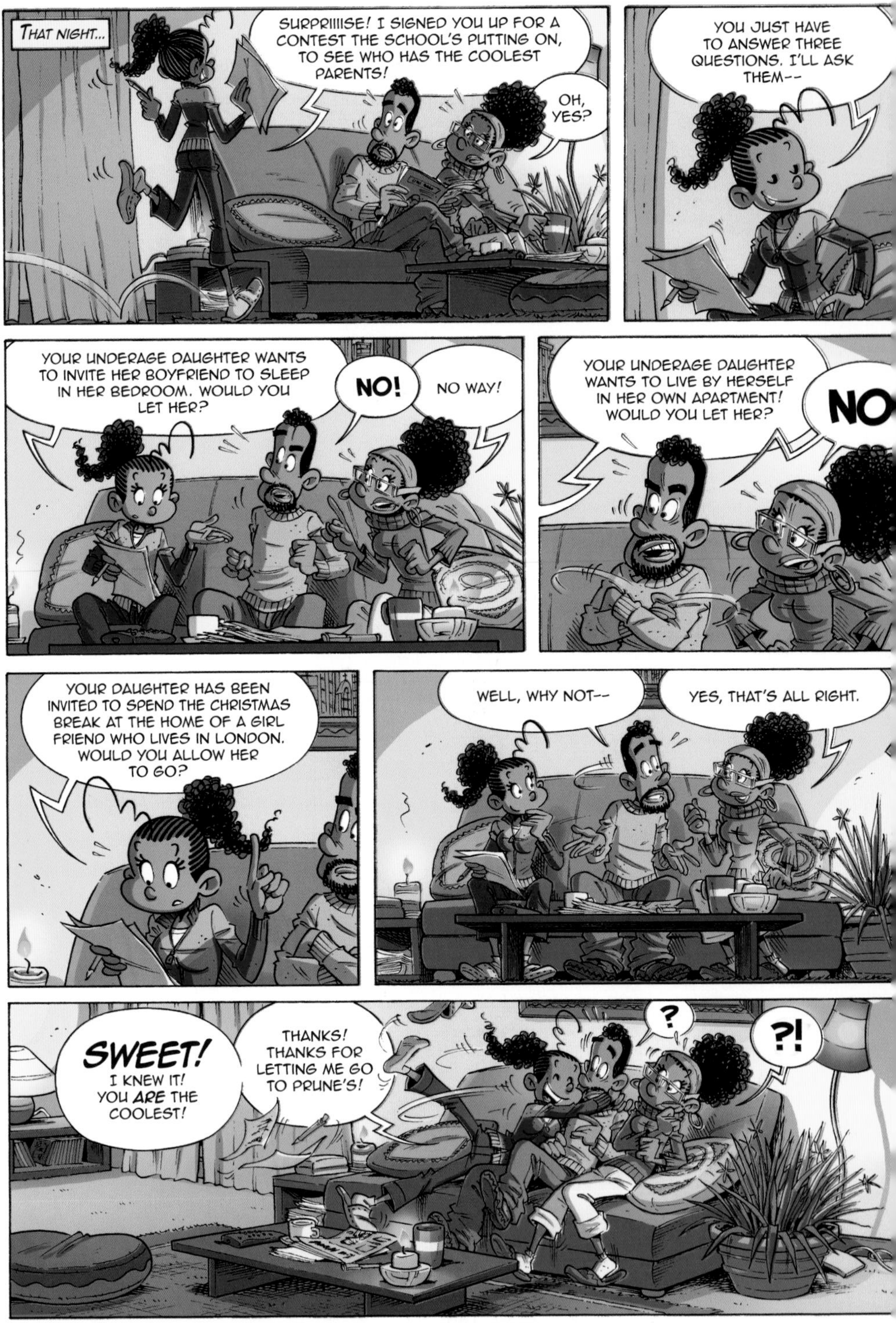
THAT NIGHT...
SURPRIIIIISE! I SIGNED YOU UP FOR A CONTEST THE SCHOOL'S PUTTING ON, TO SEE WHO HAS THE COOLEST PARENTS!
OH, YES?
YOU JUST HAVE TO ANSWER THREE QUESTIONS. I'LL ASK THEM--
YOUR UNDERAGE DAUGHTER WANTS TO INVITE HER BOYFRIEND TO SLEEP IN HER BEDROOM. WOULD YOU LET HER?
NO!
NO WAY!
YOUR UNDERAGE DAUGHTER WANTS TO LIVE BY HERSELF IN HER OWN APARTMENT! WOULD YOU LET HER?
NO
YOUR DAUGHTER HAS BEEN INVITED TO SPEND THE CHRISTMAS BREAK AT THE HOME OF A GIRL FRIEND WHO LIVES IN LONDON. WOULD YOU ALLOW HER TO GO?
WELL, WHY NOT--
YES, THAT'S ALL RIGHT.
SWEET! I KNEW IT! YOU ARE THE COOLEST!
THANKS! THANKS FOR LETTING ME GO TO PRUNE'S!
?
?!

DON'T MISS DANCE CLASS #6 "A MERRY OLDE CHRISTMAS" – COMING SOON!

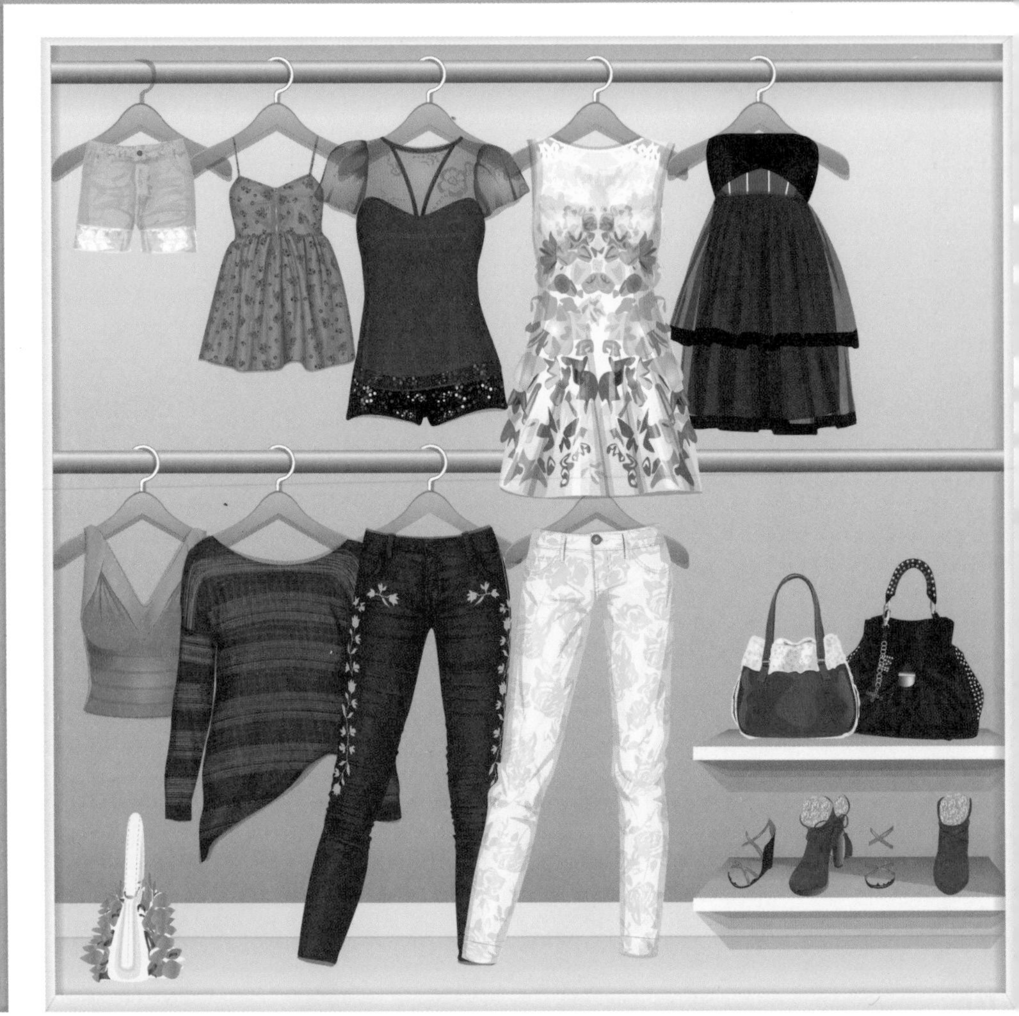